Darren Groth is a Brisbane boy transplanted to Vancouver, Canada. He is the author of acclaimed fiction novels MVP – Most Valuable Potential and The Procrastinator. MVP – Most Valuable Potential was shortlisted in the Queensland Premier's Literary Awards and was selected for the prestigious 'Books From Our Backyard: 100 Must-Read Books From Queensland' list. ***The Umbilical Word*** *is his third novel.*

Darren has appeared at numerous literary events including the Brisbane Writers' Festival and the National Young Writers' Festival. He has been a guest speaker, workshop/masterclass facilitator and writer-in-residence for literary organisations, writing groups, schools and libraries. He remains a registered Mentor with the Australian Society of Authors.

When he's not watching Family Guy with his beautiful Canadian wife, he's head-banging to Spiderbait with his six year old twins.

The Literature Series ***showcases the best Australian literary talent and is available in digital and print form.***

The Umbilical Word

Darren Groth

Interactive Press
Brisbane

Interactive Press
an imprint of Interactive Publications
Treetop Studio • 9 Kuhler Court
Carindale, Queensland, Australia 4152
sales@ipoz.biz
www.ipoz.biz/ip/ip.htm

First published by Interactive Publications, 2008

Printed in 12 pt Book Antiqua on 14 pt Bodini by Konway Printhouse, Kuala Lumpur.

National Library of Australia
Cataloguing-in-Publication data:

Author:	Groth, Darren
Title:	The umbilical word
Publisher:	Carindale, Qld. : Interactive Press, 2008
ISBN	9781876819798 (pbk.).
Dewey Number:	A823.4

To my beautiful wife Wendy, and our pair of umbilicals.

Acknowledgments

Jacket Image: *Nuno Silva, "Rounded"*

Jacket Design: *David Reiter*

Author Photos: *Jessica Ng*

Thanks go to all these folk for their help, great or small, deliberate or unintended: Simon, Des, Kath, Sean, Tara Wynne, Nick Earls, Veny Armanno, Ben Elton, The Milpera Manuscript Appraisers and the Wesley Hospital.

Contents

The Umbilical Word

Foreword

People everywhere are asking me one question: 'What's most important in life?'

It's a biggie, isn't it? Huge. Traditionally, a close third on my All-Star Big Question chart, right behind 'What happens when I die?' and 'Is Elvis still alive?' Of late though, number one with a bullet. 'What's most important in life?'—undisputed top of the pops.

Why is it so popular? Well, you people were living in a haze for a while there. Not everybody of course. Not even the majority. Just a notable few twisting the idea of what really matters into a funny shape. And then CRASH! BANG! BOOM! Things that mattered didn't matter any more. Things that meant something lost all meaning. A lot of voices I hadn't heard from in a long time were suddenly back in my ear:

"Tell me my purpose..."

"Point us the way..."

"Whassit all about then, ay?"

Perspective had come back in a mighty big hurry. And that puts 'What's most important in life?' at the head of the wish-list every time.

Okay, so what's the answer? What *is* most important in life? Well, let me make you an offer you can't refuse—a personalised response to your query! The message sent will carry my very own signature. Friends and relatives may see it as something else, perhaps dumb luck or coincidence. Maybe even common sense. Discerning customers will recognise the truth.

But wait—there's more! For a limited time only you also get this hand-crafted, beautifully finished, a-must-for-every-home, special little something from yours truly:

A miracle!

There's no number to call, no contract to sign and no minimum monthly payment. Simply follow me now, down, down, out of the sky and across the sea, over the once-welcoming shores of Australia and into the somnolent city of Brisbane, through suburbs struck dumb by the late January summer heat, until you reach New Farm—the chatty, chirpy child refusing to put the head down at nap time—down James Street for 150 houses, up the stairs of a compact timber house with concrete stumps underneath and a corrugated iron roof on top, and into the small living room where Adam and Madeline O'Doherty are watching a documentary of a professional tennis coach's efforts to mould his prepubescent daughter into a rich, articulate, unbeatable superstar.

Witness their miracle and discover what's most important in life.

Then I'll let you know where The King's been hiding.

Emperor Self-Actualised Goes to Ground

1

"Can you believe this guy? Can you believe what he's doing to his child?"

"Lie down, babe."

"Six hours a day on a blazing hot tennis court! No school! No friends! Media training, for God's sake! It's abuse, Adam. Plain and simple."

"Maddy. Lie down."

"And listen to him—thinks he's teaching his girl what it takes to be a success…come on! That peroxide he uses must have seeped through to his brain!"

Adam got up from the recliner and stood in front of his seated wife, blocking her view of the TV.

"You're not made of glass, fella," she said.

"No, but you are." He placed his hands on her shoulders and eased her back down into the couch. Maddy sniffed, tugged at a loose thread on her camouflage tank top and lifted her heels once more into the indentations on the armrest.

"I don't have to be on my back twenty-four hours a day."

"I know."

"I've got to get up sometimes."

"Yes. You do."

"I wouldn't do anything…unnecessary. I wouldn't do anything to put our little Kiddo at risk. You know that, don't you?"

"Babe, if there's one thing in this life I know, it's that."

Adam kissed his wife's forehead before issuing a 'Stay… Staaay' command and returning to the recliner. On screen,

Tennis Dad was adamant he wouldn't make his girl do anything unnecessary, anything that would put her at risk.

"Tell me you think this guy's whacked," pleaded Maddy, rolling onto her side.

"Well...."

"Oh please!"

"I think he's pretty smart."

"He makes Mariah Carey look like Peter Carey."

Adam yanked the handle at the side of his chair. A moaning, groaning footrest clunked into place. "Giving kids a head start or some sort of advantage is the way to go," he said. "I think if Dad had've taken me down to the courts as a nipper and hit a few million balls at me, then I wouldn't have lost 6-2 to Kel earlier this evening."

"Lost again, did you?"

"Yes. And all because Old Man Reg wouldn't give up putting food on the table and keeping a roof over our heads to support my dream."

"Tennis was never your dream."

"He's still a bastard."

Maddy pushed the empty, freshly disinfected spew bucket by her side to arm's distance away then plucked the remaining chunk of Mars bar off the coffee table. "So you think this is really about that child on the screen right now? You think this is all really her dream?"

"Yes. I think it is."

"You don't think that maybe this is *all* about Father Peroxide. About *his* dream?"

"Well, let's listen to what the girl says, hey?"

The flaxen-haired ten year-old wiped her brow with the sponsor's wristband, fixed her gaze and addressed the nation:

"I must stay focused, make sacrifices and work very hard if I am to achieve my lifelong goal of being number one in the world...."

Maddy ate the chocolate and shook her head. "Daddy Peroxide is good—I'll give him that. Didn't see his lips move once."

"That was all her."

"Rubbish, Adam."

"Those were her own thoughts and feelings."

"No. No! If you can't see this for what it is, then you're an idiot. A hopeless, brainwashed idiot." Maddy reached out, grasped the monstered Mars bar wrapper and held it high. "Could you possibly get me another one of these, gorgeous handsome man?"

Adam lowered the footrest and levered himself out of the recliner. Using the instep of his right foot, he nudged the spew bucket back toward the couch then retreated for the kitchen.

*

The clock near the water purifier read quarter-past nine. Adam yawned then sighed. It had come to this: if not a senior citizen's, then certainly a morning person's concept of lateness.

As recently as November he'd been recognisable, pushing past midnight on a regular basis, adding the finishing touches to his breakthrough bestseller and, in the short breaks, catching snippets of the SBS nudey shift. The mornings were never pretty—a ritual of skulling coffee heart-starters and staggering through the first two teaching periods of the day. But that was the lot of Adam O'Doherty, Night Person. Firefly by dark, dung beetle at dawn.

Eight short weeks later, the dung beetle reigned supreme. Adam couldn't stay conscious after ten and the mornings remained a tribute to caffeine and the automatic pilot.

It was inescapable. 'Being a parent changes you forever,' people told him. Well, being a *pre*-parent brought its fair share of change, too. Especially with a wife ordered to behave like a banana lounge.

Adam collected a Mars from the fridge (six still remained) then surveyed the sink and surrounding areas. The washing up needed doing tonight—the unstable sprawl constituted every piece of crockery bar the Mexican-motif dip platter and every piece of cutlery save the fondue forks. The food scraps had to be binned and the leftover tuna salad kept for Maddy's lunch tomorrow. The rest of the chores could wait until tomorrow, or the next day, or, in the case of the spaces behind the stove, the next tenants-

"Guy! Are you growing the cocoa beans in there?"

"I'm just looking for some spare insulin, babe!"

Adam scrutinised the chocolate bar. He gauged it was five times the size of his unborn child.

"Between you and me, Marsy," he said, "Madeline's going to have to earn a shot at you. Fancy criticising that bloke on TV for doing everything in his power to give his daughter the world."

"Are you talking to someone?"

"Yeah. Me. I'm a brainwashed idiot! Remember?"

"You won't have a brain to wash if you don't hot-foot it out here with that choccie!"

Adam mimed a forehand volley and flipped the kitchen light switch.

*

"You know she *is* number one in the world, for her age," served Adam, re-entering the lounge room. "She's beating seventeen and eighteen year-olds."

"Uh-huh. Seventeen and eighteen year-olds who had a childhood."

Love-fifteen. Adam tore the Mars wrapper with his teeth and spat out the plastic wedge.

"To be that good, her Dad must be doing something right."

"Yes. It's called exploitation."

Love-thirty. Adam pulled the chocolate out, scrunched the wrapper into a ball and tossed it over his shoulder.

"Look at her on screen there, Maddy. Wouldn't a child like that make you proud? Wouldn't a child like that make you happy?"

"Any child would make me happy, Adam. Any child at all."

Game, set and match. Adam placed the naked new Mars on the palm of his wife's hand, closed her fingers around it and returned to the recliner.

"Thank you, gorgeous handsome man."

*

Adam stood watch outside the closed toilet door, hands in pockets, tracing the line of the floorboards with his sandshoe. At the sound of the flush, he leapt sideways into the adjoining bathroom and scrabbled around at the sink, trying to secure his toothbrush and the toothpaste by feel alone. He held them up as Maddy's turquoise-painted toenails came into view.

"Just cleaning my teeth. Now that the washing up's done. Gunna head for bed. Are...are you okay?"

Maddy splashed water on her face. "You've got my brush."

"Oh. Sorry."

She dabbed herself with a towel. "And the eczema cream."

"Oh, shit. Sorry."

"I really wish you wouldn't stand outside the loo listening to me."

"I wasn't...listening to you. I'm just...you know, worried."

"Well, stop standing outside the loo worrying about me. Stand somewhere else and worry about me."

"Okay."

"In fact, *stop worrying about me*. It just makes me more worried. And I'm doing enough worrying for both of us, believe me."

"Right."

Maddy wound her arms around her husband's waist and laid her head against his bare chest. "You're a typical man,

Adam. A would-be Sir Fix-A-Lot."

Adam picked a sliver of Mars out of her chestnut ponytail. "I know I can't do anything to help. I know it's in the lap of the gods. It's just that…"

"What?"

"It's just that, well…I wish we had more idea of what's going on. You know? More information."

Maddy pushed herself away to arm's length. "Don't say it, Adam."

"Don't say what?"

"I'm not getting a scan done, Adam."

"Babe-"

"I'm not going to a doctor."

"I know that---"

"I'm not going down that road again—I don't care what you say!"

Adam held his hands up in surrender. "I'm not saying anything, Mad. Okay? Really, I'm not."

He moved forward a step then dropped to his knees. He kissed his wife's trembling hands for close to a minute then looked up to confirm what he'd already seen in the mind's eye: pallid face, shallow breaths, gaze through him, beyond him. He laid his cheek against her belly. Every time she suffered, he promised it would be the last time. He would promise again tonight.

God, I'm useless! he thought.

"I wasn't criticising what we're doing now," he said. "Dawn Marks is the best midwife around and you trust her. That's good enough for me, honest. I just meant…shit, *I don't know* what I meant. Maybe something crazy, like the child communicating with us. *Talking* to us. Telling us everything's okay. Something way out like that."

He gave himself two theatrical slaps across the cheek then let his hands fall by his sides.

"Sir Fix-A-Lot—I don't think so. Lord Bugger-Up more like it."

*

Maddy recognised the man at her feet. He had proposed like this, on his haunches. She'd laughed at him. One knee was love, she'd argued. Two was desperation.

He'd replied that he was desperately in love.

Nine years on, was it still the case? In her darker moments, she imagined him dashing off with some younger, thinner, better dressed chick; unscarred, History-free, who didn't demand Mars bars or inspire toilet door vigils, who could see a pregnancy through to term and, in doing so, fulfil the most basic function of the female species. And she wouldn't begrudge him his flight. Given the chance to run away from herself, she would've outpaced an Olympic sprinter.

The day-to-day evidence refuted her worst imaginings. He hugged her when she needed it. He kissed her unannounced. He cracked up at her rude puns. He got horny over her untouchable body. He eagerly reported dreams in which he remained faithful to her and he changed the channel when Halle Berry appeared on TV. He met her every requirement without overt complaint. He promised the suffering would end.

And he still got down on both knees.

*

Maddy wiped her eyes with the knuckle of her right index finger, breathed deeply and placed her hands on her husband's shoulders.

"Arise, Lord Bugger-Up."

Adam stood. He surveyed her face, searching for any residual hurt. There was none. The light had returned.

"I'm sorry," she said. "I over-reacted."

"Babe, don't be sorr-"

Maddy covered his mouth. "Just tell me we're going to make it."

"Mmmph phhmm phmmpphh."

"Tell me things will be different this time around."

"Mpphhhmm phhmmh mmph phm."

She took her hand away. "Tell me why?"

Adam waited for the sudden surge of New Farm noise—a thumping bass line, a siren, far-away yahoos with their backyard fireworks—to die down.

"Because it's meant to be," he said. "And because the Bugger-Up name must live on."

Maddy smiled and handed over the toothpaste.

"Don't scratch."

*

Adam awoke in bed, startled and uncomfortable. After a moment's adjustment to the light, he peeled the bookmark off his cheek. He extracted the big, heavy hardback—Venero Armanno's *The Volcano*—from his armpit and examined the crumpled text.

"Page one-hundred," he mumbled. "Yaaay."

He closed the book, hauled it over onto the bedside table and turned the lamp off. The bright red numbers of the digital clock radio showed 10:50. Adam had started reading page ninety-eight at 9:56. I might never finish this book, he thought, pulling the sheet up over his chest. Perhaps their child would be willing to narrate the final scenes for him at the nursing home.

Their child.

Their 'meant to be' child.

Did he really believe his own propaganda? Lying there in the dark, alone with his thoughts, absent of the need for consolation or comfort, he knew there was only one answer: absolutely. The O'Dohertys had paid their dues. They'd been force-fed patience and perseverance and providence, and now it was time for some reward. And then there was the timing of this pregnancy, too. Was it coincidence that it should occur at the same juncture as his success? Was it happenstance that their twin dreams should be fulfilled in the same year? Absolutely not. There was destiny involved here. A convergence of cosmic forces. A masterplan.

Adam snuggled up to his wife. Maddy snorted and rolled onto her side. Adam kissed her bare back.

"Things will be different alright," he whispered. "I promise."

2

The Carsmair High staff whiteboard displayed a single message:

Welcome back crew!
Write down the biggest news of your holiday in the space below!
Biggest wins life membership with Education Department!
Second biggest—HONOURARY life membership!

Adam surveyed the candidates thus far: George had finished painting the deck; Dilip had swum with the sharks at Sea World; Lynne's daughter had been accepted into NIDA; Debra's ex-husband had had to declare bankruptcy. He picked up a marker and tapped his chin.

"*Million dollar book deal,*" volunteered a voice behind him. "*Go stick your life membership up your*...mmm, how would a big shot writer put it?"

Adam thought for a second, turned and wrote his response in the air: "*Stick it up your three R's....*" He smiled at the bespectacled, blonde pixie standing by the 'Maths Stuff' filing cabinet, bouncing from foot to foot. "Jenna Grimson, my high school sweetheart."

"Adam O'Doherty, my boy behind the bike sheds." She gave him a hug then stood back, hands on hips. "So, continue please. Write your fabulous news for all to see."

Adam yanked the lid off the marker and pivoted back toward the board. Inside his head, Maddy's waking mantra pounded away like a boxer's jab:

"Don't tell."

"Don't tell!"

"DON'T TELL!"

He knew the rules: pregnancy was best revealed around the twelve week stage, at the back end of the risky first trimester. To tell any earlier invited the prospect of having to un-tell later. Thus far in the O'Doherty History the wounds had been spared such salt and, as far as Maddy was concerned, they weren't going to chance it now. Being the sole possessor of their ordeal's knowledge was her single, tiny, saving grace amidst the devastation. She also believed it was a jinx to mention the bun before the oven had even heated up.

But what about Destiny? thought Adam. A man turns up to work, firm in his resolve to stay silent, and pray tell what is the first thing encountered when he walks in? A whiteboard cum inquisitor, armed with bold print and exclamation marks and the interrogative glare of the fluorescent lights above, demanding he damn the rules and spill the beans!

An omen, for sure. And omens were not supposed to be ignored. They were adverts for the masterplan.

Adam piloted an unsteady hand toward the board---

(DON'T TELL!!!!!!!!!)

---and recorded his holiday highlight:

Caught a rocket ship to a whole new planet

Jenna brought her hands to her open mouth. "Ohmigod!" she squeaked. "Ohmigod, Adam!"

"What?"

"Congratulations!"

"What, what?"

"You did it!"

"Did what?"

"You sold your book! You nailed the career deal!" Jenna scooted over to the window and hailed the driveway statue of the school's founder and first Principal, Barry Carsmair: "HEY BAZ! GUESS WHAT! SEE THIS GUY IN HERE?"

"Jenna."

"HE NAILED IT!"

"No, I didn't."

"BIT LIKE THOSE PIGEONS WITH YOU! Sorry, what did you say?"

"I haven't nailed anything, Jay...well, not yet anyway." Adam tossed the pen in the air. "You didn't think it was a metaphor, did you?"

Jenna closed thc window, blushed, bit her bottom lip. "Writers like metaphor. 'Rocket ship'...'planet'...I thought you were being clever."

"I'm not clever."

"Oh."

Adam wrapped an arm around his friend's shoulders. "In Tristan's own words the 'irons in the fire are still heating up'."

"Is *he* clever?"

"I hope so."

"He's your agent, isn't he?"

"Apparently. He's sent it off to the six big houses. Their replies should come in over the next few months. He reckons it's a 'shoe-in'."

"Really?"

"He says my life is going to 'go ballistic'."

Jenna held her closed fists under her chin and gave a little squeal. "God Adam, it's so exciting! *I'm* excited—I can only imagine how *you* feel."

"Eh."

"What...aren't you excited?" Jenna inspected her colleague at close quarters. "You look like crap, Ad."

"I need a coffee."

"Are you worried about the submissions?"

"Nope."

"Has this Tristan fellow got the goods?"

Adam took a moment, choosing his words carefully. "I think he's a bit of a twit...but his client list certainly suggests that, yes, he has got the goods. In the end, though, what he says or does is probably irrelevant anyway. The work must stand on its own. And it will—I've no doubt."

Jenna stood silent for a moment, measuring the truth of her friend's response. "It's not the book," she conceded. "That's great. So...why are you so wrecked?"

Adam rolled the whiteboard marker between his fingers. "I'm busy at home."

"Busy."

"Maddy's a bit crook at the moment."

"Oh no. What's she got?"

"Tummy bug."

"Oh no. There's plenty of those going around."

"Yeah."

"Should I give her a ring at lunch time? Try and cheer her up a bit?"

Adam shook his head. "She's not real keen on talking right now. Wants to keep it quiet that she's, you know...sick. Hey, Boyd!"

Boyd Grimson ceased his scrutiny of the semester timetable and summoned a quick march out of his creaky footballer's legs. He gave his wife a peck on the cheek then read Adam's holiday note.

"Whole new planet, hey? Where'd you go, O'Doherty? Mars?"

Adam nodded. "Several times."

Boyd eased his wife away from the whiteboard then tapped his watch. "Staff meeting in five, boys and girls. The Sarge'll do his nana if we're late."

Adam replaced the marker in the tray. The trio headed for the library.

*

Deputy Principal Merrill Hagan, known to all and sundry at Carsmair State High School as 'The Sarge', stepped up to the podium.

"I think we might get started, troops."

After a short wait and a few shooshes, silence was achieved. The Sarge shuffled his papers, adjusted his RSL tie clip then cleared the phlegm from his throat. His right eye took in much of the seated, fifty strong staff that served under him. His left eye, turned from birth and shunned during the initial Vietnam roll call, fell upon an out-of-order photocopier at the fringe of the gathered group.

"Ladies and gentlemen," he began, "this year promises to be a call to arms. The world today is an unknown quantity. There exists a climate of uncertainty from which no nation, no institution, no individual is immune. People everywhere are grappling with feelings of anxiety and fear. For our kids — the inheritors of this world — the struggle is all the more intense, all the more confusing. What are the possibilities? What can I aspire to? What sort of future can I expect? These are the questions they have."

Adam shifted in his chair. These were the questions the students of Carsmair had? Perhaps if you took away some syllables, added some profanities, availed them of the capacity to think beyond sex and drag racing.

"Can we give them answers?" continued The Sarge. "Probably not. Can we give them anything that will help? By jingoes, yes! We can give them what all kids need, what all kids deserve: T-R-S. Trust. Respect. Security. Someone they can talk to. Someone they can listen to. Someone they know is going to be there. Someone they know is working for their benefit. Someone they want beside them as they prepare to go over the top and charge that uncertain world. T-R-S, ladies and gentlemen! The important stuff in life!"

Merrill Hagan acknowledged the smattering of applause then mopped his brow with a khaki handkerchief.

I can't do this, thought Adam.

He'd come into the school year with a plan for redemption. It would start with this student-free day staff meeting. Occupy a front row seat, sit up straight, eyes forward. Devote attention wholly and solely to work instead of the usual beach holiday, famous author, Wimbledon triumph daydreams. Such were the behaviours of other teachers, *good* teachers. Teachers who truly believed their profession to be the noblest of them all. Teachers with joy in their hearts and fire in their guts. Teachers who gave a shit about the students. Teachers like Jenna and Boyd. Vera and Cate. Lynne. And Dilip, sitting closest to the podium, leaning forward, taking notes, nodding in a manner that suggested The Sarge was a venerated *swami* and his outline of the earbashing fest to follow was a free ticket to *nirvana*. In his final year, Adam O'Doherty would be amongst them. It was the right thing to do after nine years of adequate fakery.

He'd lasted five minutes.

A shame, he thought, settling into a back row chair. But no surprise. Earthly duties didn't matter much to those who caught rocket ships to whole new planets.

Adam opened his glossy new teacher's diary to the section titled 'Staff Meeting Notes' and wrote: *'Our baby is presently one fifth the size of a Mars bar'*. He nodded. The inquisitor would be satisfied with that. So too Destiny. Talk it up, get it out there; gratefully accept the well-wishes, the handshakes, the raised glasses; soak up all the goodwill… such an atmosphere of joy and celebration could only be good, *do* good, for the little life growing inside Maddy. A cursory glance at History indicated something had been lacking in the past—perhaps telling was it? Perhaps giving voice to their unborn child was the missing piece of the jigsaw, the lucky last ball in the lottery?

Maree Kurylewski, Financial Consultant with the Education Department, now occupied the podium. She thanked Merrill Hagan for his inspiring introduction and contended that teachers couldn't provide security for their students if they didn't feel secure themselves. The most meaningful way to achieve that, she claimed, was to salary sacrifice in the interests of topping up your superannuation. Several pie graphs later, Adam got up from his chair and headed for the door. As he passed Jenna her raised eyebrows suggested he'd better have a damn good excuse.

"Something I need to do," he whispered.

He exited the conference area and headed for the staffroom whiteboard.

*

Maddy sat up and perused the coffee table. Distributed across the scratched Cypress surface were a multitude of tasks, hobbies, games, distractions and time-wasters that Adam—gorgeous handsome man!—had hurriedly organised for her during breakfast. Prior to leaving, he'd calculated their accumulated care factor to be well in excess of his seven-hour absence. Maddy looked at her watch and performed some calculations of her own.

"Only five hours short," she murmured.

In hindsight, the 'Super Fun Happy Interesting Table' as Adam had dubbed it might've benefitted from a little more thought. The 'World's Greatest Drinking Games' cards didn't trouble the scorer. Nor the Twister mat. The Nintendo Game Boy undoubtedly held the potential to propel time occupied beyond lunch—without batteries it left much to be desired. And as for the National Geographic 'Where in the World Are We?' board game...Maddy defied any person with access to growing grass or peeling wallpaper to find it diverting. Consequently, at 11.08 on the morning of her Super Fun Happy Interesting Husband's first day back at work, staring at the ceiling and its rotating fan represented much of the foreseeable future's prospective entertainment.

Maddy resumed her position on the couch. She wondered if her man was struggling to stay plugged-in himself. He had promised to approach this final year with a revised attitude—was he walking the talk? She hoped so. A return to the teacher's survival instinct, to *chalking* the talk, gave rise to an Adam desperate for distraction. And an Adam desperate for distraction might create his own.

She could empathise with that.

Hoisting a leg onto the Super Boring Crap Table, Maddy grasped the cordless phone's small antenna between her toes. After shifting the appliance to her hand, she scrolled through the bank of saved numbers. The tiny screen displayed several Adam-inspired listings: 'R&E (Mouldy Oldies)'—'Carsmair (Endsville)'—'Kel (The Other Goran)'. At the one titled 'Can Fam (Lock Up Your Moose)', she paused. Her thumb shifted left from the chunky master button to the 'Call' command. She summoned her little Kiddo with a pat of the abdomen.

"Something I need to do," she whispered.

She pressed her thumb down and waited for the seemingly endless series of beeps to fashion a relieving connection.

*

"Ladies and gentlemen…without further ado, I would like to announce the winner in our 'Biggest News of the Holidays' competition. There were many worthy candidates. Marjorie's first grandchild. David seeing himself up on the big electronic scoreboard at the cricket. Bree losing eight kilos—great effort, darl. But in the end it was no contest. A late entry blew everyone else away. Ladies and gentlemen, the provider of the biggest news of the hols, and the winner of the life membership with the Education Department, is none other than…" Jenna grasped a pair of rulers, performed a drumroll on the table then struck the proffered lid of the coffee tin, sending it spinning into the salad sandwich section of the Carsmair staff's catered lunch. "CALLUM CUTHBERT MORECROFT!"

Applause filled the common room. A chorus of cajoling eventually convinced the longest-serving teacher at Carsmair State High School to make his way toward the presentation area. He accepted his certificate. Jenna pinned the 'LIFER' badge to his chest and pressed the prison number sticker over the pocket of his Target business shirt.

"Okay, thanks. Yeah," said Morecroft. "I thought havin' an eighteen year-old daughter hook up with a thirty-two year-old bloke on the internet, fly half way round the world to meet him, and return home with a ring on her finger wasn't much chop. But this," he patted the badge, "this makes it all worthwhile."

A second ovation commenced. Callum Morecroft returned to his seat using the certificate as a napkin for a piece of garlic bread.

"Brings a tear to the eye, doesn't it?" remarked Boyd.

"Several," replied Adam.

"Do you know if he applied for the fifty grand?"

"The 'Different Employment' Scheme? No, he didn't. I overheard him talking to George."

"You're kidding." Boyd stabbed a piece of lettuce with his plastic fork. "I thought he'd be first in line for any scheme that'd get you out of the game."

"Maybe deep down he doesn't mind being a 'LIFER'."

"Ten-to-one on we find that badge in the potato salad."

At the rear of the staff room, corks began popping. Plastic cups were held out and half-filled with Seaview Grand Cuvee. A splurge! thought Adam. Perhaps someone had died and bequeathed their topped-up super to the staff social club? More likely the bottle-o had run out of Spumante.

"A toast!" cried Jenna. "To all the inmates! And, in light of our new superannuation expertise, may Carsmair become a maximum security facility!"

The dull 'thok' of plastic cup striking plastic cup punctuated the murmured salutations and polite sips. Adam noted Callum Morecroft's single gulp and subsequent sounding out of potential teetotalers.

"You reckon doing this job was ever Cal's dream?"

Boyd smacked his lips and shrugged. "Maybe. Back in the Stone Ages. You'd have to think it never was though. He probably settled for the consolation prize at some point."

"Around the time his daughter came into the world?"

"Who knows? The only thing for certain is he's not getting fifty grand from the Ed Department to pay for her wedding."

A plate filled with rice crackers, sun-dried tomatoes and feta swept into the space between the two men. Adam and Boyd looked up to find the broad, fluoride-rich, always available grin of Dilip Shastrani illuminating the offer.

"Eat up to build your energy, fellows," he said, "for you have just witnessed our futures."

Boyd took a cracker and modelled it against his chest. "When I get my badge, I'll wear it with honour." Adam plucked it away from his grasp and ate it.

Dilip put the plate on the table and stood before his colleagues, bowed, hands joined, smile momentarily short-circuited.

"Friends, please, you misunderstand. I'm referring to Cal's baby girl. Our days of teenager-inspired dismay are coming!"

"Probably not for a little while," contended Boyd. "Seeing as Adam and I don't even have kids yet."

"Ha-ha! There is a saying in India: 'The blink of an eye is the passing of an age'!"

"And you're assuming we want kids."

"Of course. They are the greatest gifts anyone can receive."

"Yeah. Just ask Cal." Boyd stretched his arms above his head and mumbled some forecasts. "I reckon family might make the priority list in about five to seven years. By then I'll be in administration, we'll have most of the house paid off, the investment property will have doubled in value and we'll have done all the travelling we want to do." He looked toward Adam. "What about you, O'Doherty? You've been married a long time. When are you going to have a kid?"

"Who's going to have a kid?" inquired Jenna, blustering into the conversation, MC duties now complete.

"No one," assured Adam.

"Dilip was just teeing us up to be parents, Jay."

Jenna extracted a seashell from the Guylian box, paused, pinched a seahorse as well. "I'm not sure children are such a good idea."

Adam almost choked on his disbelief. "Didn't you pay for your entire pastoral class to get into Dreamworld?"

"Yes."

"Didn't you regard last year's senior formal as a 'hoot'?"

"Yes."

"And didn't you say Sonny Burnside and his grade ten band were 'destined for greatness' when clearly he had a voice worse than a swarm of seagulls fighting over a discarded chip?"

"I did tell him greatness might take a while."

Adam clapped Boyd on the shoulder. "Never mind the five to seven years, mate. You've already got kids. About six hundred of them!"

Jenna sniffed and sucked the chocolate off her fingers. "Responsibility for my students is easy. Responsibility for my own child…I'm not sure I want that. Particularly given the way the world is right now."

"You've been listening to The Sarge too long."

"And anyway there's things I still want to do." She closed in to within an inch or two of Adam's face, eyes wide and slightly magnified behind the lenses of her bright red Jag frames. "I want to be a writer!"

"Good for you."

"Did you notice my metaphor up there? The whole prison thing. 'Inmates'. 'Maximum security'."

"I think that was more like pathos."

"Really? Well I think you're totally pathos, chum!" Jenna walked over to the whiteboard and pointed to the blank space between Arnold Parkthorn's purchase of a campervan and Deirdre Mengel's bowling a two hundred game. "Where'd the 'rocket ship' and the 'whole new planet' go?"

"I had to rub it out," confessed Adam. "It was being misinterpreted. People were thinking it was clever. They were getting all keyed up and dancing around and yelling out at marble statues in the driveway. Acting like total yobs they were. Couldn't have that sort of behaviour on the first day back."

"Tell the truth, O'Doherty," said Boyd, presenting his friend and colleague of seven years with a rice cracker. "You were afraid you might win."

"Or come second," added Dilip.

Adam looked over toward Callum Morecroft, now seated at his desk. Several empty cups were scattered amongst the papers. A breeze filtered through the open window and ruffled the greyed temples of his otherwise dyed head of hair. He appeared to sway.

The 'LIFER' badge was gone.

*

Adam opened the driver-side door of the Rav 4 and stepped onto the grass bordering the 150 James Street driveway. He looked in the direction of the mailbox. Visions of the past came to him; brisk approaches filled with anticipation, rummaging hands, publisher's contract fantasies, pizza voucher realities. The warped wooden cylinder had once been the site of Hope's eternal wellspring. These days it was dry. The phone, e-mail—they were the new oases. Sometime soon, one or both would offer up news of everlasting change and all-conquering achievement. Adam turned on his heel and took the front stairs two at a time. It felt mighty good to be moving up in the world.

Inside the house, Maddy was lying on the couch, half-buried by a hoard of very long, very thin strips of white wax paper.

"Mintie wrappers," she revealed. "I had one of those 'It's moments like these… ' moments this morning."

"Just the one?"

"It was the mother of all moments."

"Uh-huh. Good thing we had that jumbo bag left over from New Year's." Adam shooed a small tumbleweed off the adjacent dining chair and sat down. "And you wanted to shred the evidence?"

Maddy yawned and stretched her arms above her head. "You remember that contest back when we were kids? The one where you had to tear a Mintie wrapper into one long continuous strip?"

"They're running it again, are they?"

"I don't think so. No, I just felt it would be a more productive use of my time than self-harming. Here! Have a look at this one!" Maddy held up a stringy, straggly effort that measured a metre and a half plus. "Impressive, hey?"

"It is actually."

"I want Kiddo to see that one. Evidence of my dedication to the cause."

Adam nodded, took it from her and hung it over the CD tower. He then noted the bare coffee table. "Didn't live up to the hype I gather."

"Not quite."

"Is there anything in the house you haven't read yet?"

"Uh-huh. The user guides and warranties."

"I'll pick up some Super Fun Happy Interesting books from the library tomorrow."

"Thank you, gorgeous handsome man."

Adam began clumping the remaining, expendable Mintie wrapper strands into a bin-friendly ball. "Any calls today?"

"I rang home. Mum said it was snowing in Vancouver."

"Did you mention anything about…us?"

"No. Did you?"

"Of course not."

"Well that's good then." Maddy scratched her cheek, averted her eyes.

Maybe she feels guilty about this morning, thought Adam. Ashamed she didn't trust me, that she said 'Don't tell!' enough times for all the secrets of the world to remain safe. He recalled the sentence he'd scribbled in his diary. At some point in the evening, he would remove the offending page and tear it up like so much lolly wrapper.

"Your Mum rang, too," continued Maddy. "The birthday barbecue for Reg is Sunday week."

"Do you know what he told Shelley he wanted for a present?"

"No."

"A grandchild."

Maddy pressed the volume button on the TV remote. "We'll buy him some Guinness."

Adam gathered a soccer ball-sized nest of paper up into his arms and, following his wife's suggestion, dumped it in the spew bucket. Stray strands hung on the rim and over the sides.

"You can manage without this for two minutes?" he asked.

"If I get desperate, I'll use your briefcase."

Tendrils trailing behind, Adam entered the kitchen. He stamped the pedal bin. As the lid flew up, revealing a sorry clutch of Fantale debris, Maddy called out from the lounge:

"Oh, Tristan rang, too."

Adam emptied the bucket, brought the teetering mound to heel with a single stomp from his Colorado boot, and tied the handles of the garbage bag. His spine tingled. His heart bounced around his ribcage. His head swam with all manner of triumphant scenarios. He exited the kitchen with the bucket held against his right hip.

"He left a message. It's number three."

Adam deposited the bucket on the coffee table and headed for the blinking answer machine. He pressed 'Play' then skipped over Maddy's three year-old niece sharing the news that she'd gone to the toilet to 'drop some friends off at the pool' and Kelly Clark belting out a rendition of The Proclaimers' '500 Miles' that sounded more Pakistani than Scottish. The husky American residing in the machine announced the time and date for message three. Adam noted the minutiae of the scene around him. The small wicker basket filled with twenty and fifty cent pieces. The grass-caked sandshoes used for mowing the lawn. The wooden doorstop, chewed by the Ridgeback of a house-minding friend. Details for when Rove asked him about *that* phone call.

"Adam, hello. Hello to Mandy, too. It's Tristan here. Just

wanted to make sure you were busy, busy, beavering away on the next story. I was thinking when *The Ordinary Man's Enemy* lands a deal, we might be able to negotiate an advance on the new masterpiece. That'd be out-standing, wouldn't it? One way or the other, it's all good. Let me know at some stage what you're working on. Busy, busy! Okay…Ciao."

Adam pressed 'Stop' and leaned against the wall. Maddy was standing at the entrance to the corridor.

"Bad news?"

He shook his head.

"Not the news you were hoping for though."

He shrugged. "When it lands a deal, negotiating an advance on a new novel…it's all good. Apart from the fact there is no new novel. Not even an idea."

Maddy took her husband's hand. "I'm sorry."

"What for?"

"For being…high maintenance."

"You're not high maintenance." Adam sat down on a nearby chair and manoeuvred Maddy onto his knee. "You're not stopping me doing stuff. I just don't…want to write anything at the moment."

"How come?"

Adam laughed. "It probably sounds a bit dumb but I feel like I need permission. I feel like I can't really justify starting something else until the breakthrough has happened. Until I've proven my worth. Does that sound dumb?"

"Yes. It does. If you'd started out that way, you never would've written anything."

Adam began chewing the fingernail of his right pinkie. Maddy gently extracted the digit from his mouth. "I don't know," he said. "Maybe I'm focusing too much on stuff I can't control."

"Maybe you're right."

"Maybe I'm a control freak."

"King Control Freak."

"I thought I was Sir Fix-A-Lot, alias Lord Bugger-Up?"

"You're moving up in the world."

*

Adam was sitting in the recliner, revising lessons for the first school day of the year, wondering if the grade ten Citizenship Education students might take to a session on the virtues of salary sacrifice, when Maddy tugged on his sleeve:

"Come with me."

"Babe, you really shouldn't be getting up again."

"This is important."

Maddy led him into the spare room. She urged him to sit at the computer then placed an open book on the desk in front. Adam turned it over. The cover read: *Fathering the Foetus – How to Be a Great Dad for Your Unborn Child!* The author was Professor Emmett G. Bragg. The cover photo displayed a mawkish mid-fifties man, no doubt the good Prof, offering a high-five to an anonymous pregnant woman's bulge.

"When did you get this?"

"Last Friday. Read the passage I've marked."

"How did you get this?"

"I ordered it through the net. Read the passage."

"*Why* did you get this?"

"Read the passage or I'll send you out to buy more Minties."

Adam rubbed his forehead, flipped the book open and read the highlighted paragraph aloud:

"'*It is often in the eighth week of the pregnancy that the reality of impending fatherhood begins to hit home and it is at this stage that fathers feel disempowered. A common technique for Dads-to-be to self-validate is to write a letter, a message, perhaps even an e-mail to their unborn child. The act of writing provides a sense of control and often reveals thoughts and feelings men do not generally air. Such honesty with yourself will set you on the path to embracing and self-actualising the personification of your fatherhood role.*' I'm assuming you didn't show me this for its entertainment value."

Maddy clicked the mouse and pulled the keyboard out. "This is something you can control. You said last night you wanted communication with our child? Here's your chance, Your Majesty. Say all the things you want to say. Ask all the things you want to know. Put it all out there. You'll feel better for it."

'So let's tell everyone we're pregnant then.' Adam felt these words take shape in his mouth, but swallowed before they could be aired. Instead he asked: "What do I do with it when it's written?"

"Whatever you like. Delete it. Save it. It doesn't matter. It's the act of doing it that's important. You could print it and stick it in an envelope."

"Mail it? You might want to have a few drinks before I try that."

Maddy slapped the back of his skull. "The other good thing about it is that you'd be writing. It's not a new story, but it is creative. And it could be good fun."

Adam smoothed the hair roughed up by Maddy's blow and looked again at the book cover. What would Emmett G. Bragg have written to his child? *'In the interests of personifying and self-actualising my fatherhood, I just had to slap some skin with you, Junior! Sorry about the brain damage!'*

"What about the washing," he said. "Didn't you say you'd run out of undies?"

"This takes precedence."

"Precedence over undies?"

"Precedence over housework. The undie situation-" she pulled down the belt line of her cargo three-quarters, revealing the Carbon and Boron elements of Adam's Periodic Table boxer shorts, "is under control."

Adam handed *Fathering the Foetus* back and rolled the mouse around on the Ouija board pad. For the second time today, a white screen was in his face. A more subtle inquisitor this one. With his wife's weight thrown behind it, impossible to resist. He edged his chair forward and flicked the miniature dreamcatcher hanging off the top right corner of the monitor. He then laid his hands on the keyboard.

Maddy squeezed his shoulder, kissed the crown of his head and exited the room.

*

From: "Adam O'Doherty" <edam_odoh@fathertobe.com>
To: "Tin Lid" <womb@almighty.com>
Subject: Um...Hello

Dear Child

I'm not sure the way of the world ought to be questioned like this, but circumstances have persuaded me to put my hand up.

Hi. I'm your Dad.

You're probably surprised, maybe even shocked by my nosiness in contacting you at this early stage. You're probably thinking 'If this guy won't give me any peace eight weeks after conception, then we may as well have the therapist on hand in the delivery room'.

I'm sorry. It is not my intention to make you uncomfortable. That's the last thing I would want to do right now. I simply wanted to make sure there are no problems and, if we're in the clear, maybe I could give you a little preview of this merry-go-round called Life.

Are there any problems? Are you feeling good? Strong? Maddy (your Mum) conceded yesterday that things felt 'different' this time around. She's still nervous as all hell, but it warmed my heart to hear her say something positive. And Dawn Marks, our midwife, has had nothing but positives to say thus far. She reckons you're in 'fine shape'.

Are you in fine shape?

Looking forward to your reply.

Adam (Dad)

*

Adam leaned back in his chair.

"King Control Freak no more," he murmured. "Call me Emperor Self-Actualised."

Still reclined, he shifted and clicked the mouse. 'Save As' requested a name for his new file. What to call this? 'A Pre-Labour Letter'? 'Nil by Post'? Perhaps something Bragg-esque: 'I Am Father—Hear Me Roar'? He looked around the room for inspiration then returned to the shirtless, angular frame stretched out before him.

"Perfect."

He picked the lint out of his navel, typed in 'The Umbilical

Word', saved then shut the computer down.

The burble of the late news on the portable TV and the tremors of a rotating pedestal fan greeted his entry to the bedroom. In spite of the noise, Maddy was crashed. The right side of her face was tattooed to her pillow whilst her arms clung to his Tontine like it was a life buoy. Adam blew her a kiss and mouthed the words 'thank you'. He turned the TV off, dropped his cut-off jean shorts and climbed into bed. After an unsuccessful attempt to retrieve his pillow, he read twenty pages of *The Volcano*—perhaps the sequel would be his nursing home tome?—then turned his bedside lamp off.

The alarm clock read 10:58.

Adam's final thought before sleep was that a high-five to Maddy's tummy would self-actualise a knee to the testicles.

3

The early morning sun streamed through the frosty glass of the spare room's only window. The angle of the rays, coupled with the passage permitted by the gaping wooden slats of the attached blind, saw much of the light fall upon the computer work-station. It was radiant. The fake white pine finish distributed fuzzy halos all around the room. The glare spuming from the monitor made sighting the screen nigh impossible. Adam O'Doherty, sitting at the station, holding a worksheet he had intended to upload to school, the very same worksheet that was now so much meaningless drivel, appeared to have no problem whatsoever. His eyes were wide. His gaze was fixed. He had hardly blinked in the half hour he'd been online.

"This is a joke," he said. "It must be a joke."

After a seventh read-through of the text on screen, Adam rose from the chair and returned to the main bedroom. Maddy was still asleep. She lay at the edge of the mattress, on her side, right arm pulled across her body and hovering out over the edge of the bed, left arm wrapped around her as-yet-unexpanded midriff. Adam got down on both knees and squeezed her suspended hand. When she failed to stir, he gave her shoulder a nudge. The hanging arm jerked back into a position that covered its counterpart and criss-crossed the abdomen. The eyelids remained shut.

"Go have a shower," she mumbled. "I can get my own breakfast."

"Did you send me a message?"

"Huh?"

"Did you send a message to my mailbox? This morning or…during the night?"

Maddy opened one eye. "You're joking."

"You did get up during the night though, didn't you?"

"Yes. For a pee."

"Did you go on the computer?"

"No. I went on the toilet as usual."

"Maddy."

"I did *not* go on the computer. I had a pee then came straight back to bed."

"Are you sure?"

"Yes, Adam. I am." Maddy lifted the sheet. "How about you, Kiddo? Did you sneak out last night for a play around with Daddy's documents? Have a little surf of the net? A wee hack-attack?" She yawned and rolled over.

Adam twitched and fidgeted. He needed her to come clean. He needed a logical explanation. Tell me you did get on the computer, babe. Tell me you had a sneaky peek at my files. Tell me you wanted to totally mess with my mind. And, please, for God's sake, tell me how you managed to e-mail me about a file you've never seen, from an address that can't be found, as a person not yet in existence. Adam nudged her again.

"What *are* you doing, fella?"

"I'm sorry. I'm sorry."

"What *is* it?"

"I just wanted to say…that…well, I won't be mad or anything. You know? If you…you know, tell me the truth."

The pedestal fan juddered as Maddy squinted at her husband of nine years. He was a child. A child claiming to be sick on the day of the big test. She shook her head. "Don't worry, Kiddo," she said rolling over once more. "Your Daddy isn't barking mad all the time. Just when he's got to go back to school. Good thing it's his last hurrah."

A minute's silence was interrupted by the first, wispy snores of Maddy's renewed sleep. Adam considered a third nudge, but refrained. He rubbed the back of his neck and retreated.

The light inside the spare room had intensified. *Fathering the Foetus* – the instigator of Adam's bafflement – was one of several shining glossies on the top row of the bookshelf, to the right of the computer station. Adam snatched it up and scanned through the contents on page three.

No chapter about *replies*.

"How about a low-five, Prof?" he said and punted the 'Number One New York Times Bestseller!' into a corner box filled with spare coat hangers.

At the desk, a pewter bottle opener in the shape of Singapore's half-lion, half-serpent guardian (Reg O'Doherty had given it to his eldest son as a lucky charm for his writing) burned white hot, causing Adam to shield his eyes as he sat down. He moved the souvenir to a shaded spot and glanced at his watch. He would be late. The standard excuses – malfunctioning alarms, domestic emergencies, traffic chaos, lethargy, indifference, disenchantment – he would've traded the current circumstances for any one of those. They were weak and unprofessional.

And completely plausible.

"This is a joke," he said, reading the message through for the eighth time. "It *must* be a joke."

*

From: "Tin Lid" <womb@almighty.com>
To: "Adam O'Doherty" <edam_odoh@fathertobe.com>
Subject: RE: Um...hello.

Dad

Hey, thanks for your message! Reading's not my strong suit right now, so The Guv helped me piece it together. Helping me with the typing, too, as it happens, despite only coming in at around 40 words per minute. Omniscient, but not good enough to be a temp apparently.

As far as I can tell there are no problems. I'm feeling good, strong. Not sure I have much shape at the moment, but what there is of it I think is fine.

A Life preview? Wicked! Tell me what's outside the bubble!

B

*

Adam sat alone at the staff table, staring at the printout. Lunch—the last scrapings of Monday night's stir-fry—lay before him, untouched in the fifteen minutes since its emergence from the microwave. To his right, the clock above the reconditioned Westinghouse fridge ticked over to twenty-past twelve. To his left, the staff whiteboard warned of a fire drill in the next week. Beyond the common room, Carsmair State High School huffed and puffed in the throes of Day One, Teaching Period Four, establishing routines, defining expectations, forgetting holidays, counting minutes till the bell.

"What the hell do I do now?" he asked, looking toward the ceiling.

"You could assist me in getting my year nines to fall in love with algebra."

Adam felt a hand on his shoulder. He snatched up the e-mail, folded it into quarters and tucked it into his breast pocket. As he observed Dilip Shastrani move to the other side of the table and sit in the chair opposite, responses to the inevitable inquiry flooded his mind: *'The paper?...It's a lesson plan...It's my union dues...It's a chain letter...It's the Magna Carta...It's the last will and testament of my much-loved, much-misunderstood Great Aunt Herbie O'Doherty...What paper?'*

"It is a fortunate man," remarked Dilip, "who can ask 'What the hell do I do now?' on the first day back."

Adam drummed his fingers on the table. He needed to appear mildly affronted instead of desperately relieved. "You don't seem to be working too hard yourself, mate."

"I don't consider what I do to be work."

"Wish I could say the same."

"Ah, you will one day." Dilip placed a fist against his heart. "The writer's dream will become reality soon."

"You sound pretty sure of yourself."

"Aren't *you* sure of yourself?"

"When it comes to the writer's dream, I am." Adam felt

the folded paper in his pocket shift with each breath. "As for everything else...."

Dilip smiled and joined his hands. "We have a saying in India: 'When the largest elephant leads, those behind are taken care of'."

A gust of wind burrowed in amongst the pile of daily newspapers at the edge of the table. The front page of the top copy stood to attention, allowing Adam a brief, sideways view of the lead stories. There were no surprises. Deception, blame, hypocrisy, cynicism, conflict and a very fat pet, ranked together in a parade of columns and captions. The Sarge had got it wrong—the world wasn't an unknown quantity at all. It was entirely predictable.

Wasn't it?

"Do you believe in miracles?" asked Adam.

"Miracles..." Dilip nodded slowly then with startling vigour. "Of course! In fact, I witnessed one just last night!"

"Hey?"

"Yes. There was an Indian movie on SBS—*'Karan Arjun'*. Did you happen to see it?"

"No. I was...otherwise occupied."

"Oh my word! Irrefutable evidence of the divine!" Dilip raised his hands toward the ceiling then brought them together in front of his chest. "Karan Arjun—they're the heroes—their uncle is a nasty dictator type person, so Mum flees with them and raises them far away. A little bit later, Karan Arjun's grandfather dies and they come to visit him. Unfortunately, the uncle gets hold of them and proceeds to---"

"Forgive and forget?" offers Adam.

"Not quite. He kicks them. He punches them. He stabs them. He drags them by horse along the desert sands for perhaps fifty miles, then he beheads them."

"I thought you said he was nasty."

"Oh, he burned what was left of them, too—I almost forgot."

"Just as well."

Dilip retreated to his desk, opened his drawer then returned with a Carsmair State High fridge magnet. "Now Adam, my friend…if you can identify the great miracle that ensues, this is yours. A lasting memento of the time before the largest elephant took the lead."

Adam performed a sign of the cross. "Okay. My guess is…they didn't die."

Dilip slid the magnet across the table then applauded. "Why write novels," he beamed, "when you could pen Bollywood epics!"

"I guess they could still dance and sing, too."

"Better than ever! And they had plenty of reason after they killed the uncle by punching dragging, beheading, etcetera."

"Ah, no hand of God for the nasty."

"He never stood a chance. Not only were his recuperative powers far less impressive, he had to tackle Arnie Schwarzenegger." Dilip made his fingers into a pair of scissors. "Nothing like a bit of creative editing."

Adam snorted and took in his first mouthful of the stir-fry lunch. "Why do people swallow that sort of thing?"

Dilip paused, ran a hand along the surface of the table. For a brief second he saw something more than his opaque reflection in the aging, polished pine.

"Because it's all they've got to eat," he replied.

He whispered something Adam interpreted as either self-admonition or prayer. He then cocked his head to one side and smiled. "Theatres in India have 'ground' seats. They are exactly what the name suggests—you sit on the dirt. At about two cents Australian, it is the only place the poorest can afford and it is always the area that is the most crowded. Now, to us, *Karan Arjun* is pathetic, even for two cents. It is ridiculous. We poke fun at it. We laugh at its 'miracles'. I have no problem with this—I think we are entitled. Especially you, Adam, the brilliant author!"

Adam smiled wanly. Dilip's earnest kudos always

pricked his ego. The man from a small country town outside Hyderabad had not read a single word of Adam's creative scribblings. Ever.

"But it is important we have understanding of other's views," continued Dilip. "To the 'ground' people, *Karan Arjun* and thousands of movies like it are not ridiculous at all. They are not far-fetched. They're not even possessive of miracles.

"*The movie itself is the miracle.*

"And it is beyond question, Adam. If heroes manage to stay alive after having their heads chopped off, that's great. If Russell Crowe suddenly appears in a gladiator's outfit or Nicole Kidman materialises on a trapeze, that's even better! The people on the ground accept their miracle, whatever implausible form it takes. They cherish it. They are grateful for it. And they pray to the gods they'll live long enough to experience it again next week."

The bell to end Period Four rang out through the undercroft and across the courtyard. Dilip checked his watch against the staffroom clock. "Playground duty," he said. "Time to play the nasty uncle!"

Adam recommended the office guillotine for any beheadings and tapped his fork thoughtfully against his cheek. He was about to resume eating when he felt Dilip's hand contact him a second time. It was pressed against his breast pocket.

"Stay grounded, my friend."

Adam watched the Indian exit the staffroom then ate lunch.

*

The spare room was as he knew it at ten to ten in the evening. The shades remained open, but the crescent moon outside the window infiltrated nothing more than the surrounding cumulus clouds. Light came courtesy of a 60 watt Philips bulb. The computer station once more resembled an Ikea knock-off.

Adam sat down on the ergonomic chair. He replaced the banished lion-serpent souvenir in its original position on the desk then double clicked the internet icon. After half a minute and several more clicks, his unborn child's message appeared before him. He moved the cursor onto the 'Send' command. Should he reply directly from his mailbox? Announce his acceptance of the miracle across the length and breadth of cyberspace? Or should he cave in to the small but niggly advisor in the back of his head, the one insisting he just hit the 'Delete' key and book himself into the nearest psychiatric facility? Adam lifted an index finger to his lips, produced a series of 'ubba-ubba' sounds then closed the screen.

"It's got to go the same way," he murmured, summoning what he would later call 'logic'. "That way I know it's…on the level."

The 'Umbilical Word' file was now open. Adam scrolled down to the document's end. There were no alterations. No additions. No mark of the divine. Emperor Self-Actualised's work remained as it was yesterday—breezy, honest, entirely oblivious to its true connotations. He typed a single asterisk under the sign-off before double-spacing the cursor, readying for a new entry. He then tilted the monitor forward, slid the ergonomic chair out from under him and placed the keyboard at his feet. A pause of several seconds and a quick scan of the senses indicated the refurbishing had not jeopardised his plan. Valuable equipment was still in working order. The house still had electricity. Maddy's gentle snoring continued uninterrupted in the adjoining room.

Satisfied, Adam O'Doherty sat on the floor—his 'ground' seat—and began to type.

*

From: "Adam O'Doherty" <edam_odoh@fathertobe.com>
To: "Tin Lid" <womb@almighty.com>
Subject: Hello again.

B

Overjoyed to read you're okay. This time around *will* be different—your reply has already confirmed that! And don't fret too much about the shape situation. You might resemble a shrimp right now (I saw a 'Nine Week' photo in a medical journal), but you'll be a big fish soon enough.

Regarding the outside, there is much important stuff to be passed on. Why deodorant is necessary. Why body piercing is not. Why mangoes should be eaten in the bathtub and why Powderfinger should be turned up to eleven. Why a staple social diet usually consists of soft-boiled relatives and half-baked friends. And why all good things come to those who persevere.

We'll take it as it comes.

Dad

Staying Mum

4

The man in the tuxedo apron took charge of the barbecue as the audience of seven held their breath. Wielding the gleaming new spatula that had emerged from leftover Christmas wrapping ten minutes before, he flipped a rissole from the hotplate to the enamel serving dish balancing on his left hand. The onlookers oohed. The act was repeated, flip heightened, hot plate to dish distance extended. The onlookers aahed. Of the ensuing ten sorties, eight hit the mark. The two misses barely touched concrete before the salivating border collie at the man's side gulped them down. The cook then made his way over, cuing the onlookers to rise.

"HAAAAAAAAAAAAAAAAA...HAPPY BIRTHDAY TO YOU, HAPPY BIRTHDAY TO YOU, HAPPY BIRTHDAY DEAR REGGIE, DAD, UNCLE DAD, MR O'DOHERTY, WOOF-WOOF, OLD BUGGER...HAAAAAAAAPPY BIRTHDAY TO YOU! HIP-HIP!"

"HOORAY!"

"HIP-HIP!"

"HOORAY!"

"HIPPITY-HIP!"

"HOORAY!"

The table seven resumed their seats as whistles and shouts of 'Speech! Speech!' did the rounds. Reginald Maurice O'Doherty nodded toward the loudest hailer—one of only two unrelated invitees—and emptied his hands. He removed his 'What's Burnin'?' chef's hat and patted down the generous thatch of hair that belied his vintage.

"Good on you, Kelly," he said. "Always proud to have you and Sandy—the mighty Clark couple!—as my Clayton's Kids."

Kelly blew several kisses. Reg O'Doherty's two 'blood' sons pretended to stick fingers down their throats.

"Apart from our sweet Madeline, it's wonderful to have all the family here for my fifty-ninth," continued Reg. "Hopefully there might be…" He glanced at Eileen, his wife of thirty-six years. She had her fingers crossed. "…one or two more for the big Six-Oh."

All eye contact between the O'Doherty parents and their children ceased. Michelle spread her napkin out and placed it on her lap. Chris whistled, prompting the border collie to sprint over and sniff around the younger master's feet. Adam took a pull on his beer.

"I'm certainly practicing," announced Kelly, noting the surrounding evasiveness.

"It doesn't work on your own," replied Sandy.

Reg picked up the spatula and waved it like a magic wand. "So get cracking you lot!"

As the man of the hour retired once more to the barbecue, Chris gave his assessment:

"Bit more verbose this year—clear sign of desperation."

"We are not desperate, Christopher," countered Eileen.

"Yeah right! How many World Vision kids have you sponsored now? Four, isn't it?"

"That's not necessarily a sign of desperation."

"True. It could be that you and Dad are just nicer and more caring than the lightweights who take on one measly child. Or you want to put Rebecca Gibney out of a job. But then what do you say about this?" Chris disappeared into the bar area then returned with a framed photograph which he placed on the table. It showed a smiling Reg and Eileen standing in front of the Big Pineapple. Glued in beside them was a cut-out of an African boy, no more than ten years of age. His hands were clasped together in front of his waist. His shoulders sagged forward. His head tilted down and left. He was embarrassed, and Kelly understood why:

"If that photo's to scale, then that kid's about fifty foot high!" He took Eileen by the hand. "These World Vision shonks are using your money for steroids, Aunty Mum."

"I stuck Samuel in that shot only because his village is trying to make a go of farming pineapples."

"They should make a go of a basketball team," declared Michelle.

"But that's not the full extent of the desperation, ladies and gentlemen," said Chris, pressing home the advantage, "Mother Dearest, is it, or is it not true, that you are calling Shelley's new golden retriever puppy the 'grand-dog'?"

Eileen snatched up the framed photo and frowned at her youngest son. "You're out of the will, Christopher...again." She addressed the entire group, Big Pineapple and Mutant Samuel held to her chest. "Okay, we *are* desperate. All our friends, relatives—they're all blessed-"

"They're all lucky bastards," interjected Reg, turning over the onions.

"They carry photos of their grandchildren and talk about their babysitting or their trips out shopping. They even show us the perk stains on their clothes! When they ask when ours are coming, all we can do is smile and say 'Sometime soon!'. It's awful!"

"It *is* awful," agreed Kelly. He gave his Aunty Mum a hug then cast a stern eye in the direction of his 'siblings'. "Well, come on. There must be something you can say to ease these people's suffering? To give them some hope? Hey?"

Michelle began buttering bread rolls. "James and I have discussed it, haven't we James?" James shrugged and continued reading the sporting trivia questions on the inside of the beer bottle caps. "I mean, Medicine and becoming an obstetrician, that's the number one priority for me right now. Getting into that changes everything. But there's never a right time to have a child is there? Just a time. If our time was in the next year...well that wouldn't be the worst thing in the world, would it?"

"That's encouraging," said Kelly, nodding toward Eileen. "Chris?"

"I hereby dedicate this month to the pursuit of a second date."

"Excellent! Righto, Edam. We all know your wife's at home crook. Is it because she's preggers? That'll certainly make your folks feel better."

Adam felt the hand of the imaginary Maddy—a 'Make Sure' Maddy—at his side clamp down on his thigh, nails digging. Easy babe, he assured her. No need for the follow-up kick to send his shins into next week.

Though it would be fitting. The least of what he deserved in light of his gaffe two days earlier.

*

From: "Adam O'Doherty" <edam_odoh@fathertobe.com>
To: "Tin Lid" <womb@almighty.com>
Subject: Blab

I told a complete stranger about you this afternoon. An elderly woman in Coles. We were at the checkout, she with her trolley of canned everything and me with an armful of pregnancy essentials (on this day—organic mince, spring water and a box of Magnum ice-creams), idly gazing at the same tabloid and its cover story "Sprogs Of The Stars".

"Babies are in fashion," she said.

I nodded, exhaled and blurted out that I was having a baby myself. She looked me up and down, then tapped the front page of the mag.

"You'll make the cover next month."

I hadn't intended to say anything—we're not supposed to be telling *anyone* right now. Don't tell your mother. She's adamant I'll succumb to the grandparental pining at Reg's 59th this weekend. Given my knee-jerk with Mrs Tin Food, her concern is probably justified.

I will sign off now. Apparently you need a Magnum.

Love

Dad

*

"All I can say is when it happens, Mum and Dad, you'll be the first to know."

As the legitimacy of such a claim became a point of debate ("What about the other grandparents...? How about the examining doctor...? To really and truly honour that statement, wouldn't they have to be present at the moment of conception...? EEEEWWWWW...!"), the grip on Adam's leg subsided. He glanced at Make Sure Maddy. She was fuelling the banter, nodding with each speaker, turning her head with each verbal volley, laughing at the barrage of jokes. Absolved of closer scrutiny, she was at ease. A satisfactory deflection had been engineered and the danger had passed. King Control Freak had managed to let one slide.

Adam drank the remainder of his beer and wondered if his child might already be seeking a father refund.

*

Maddy ceased staring at the ceiling and reached for the warbling cordless phone on the coffee table.

"Talk to me."

"Mrs O'Doherty?"

"Yes."

"Hello. How are you today?"

"I'm fabulous. How are you?"

"Good, Mrs O'Doherty, good."

"Well, that's good then."

It was a sunny voice at the other end, youthful and chipper, chock full of bite-size, easily swallowed, easily digested life experiences. It was unrecognisable to Maddy.

"Mrs O'Doherty, I was wondering if you were interested in cheaper phone calls?"

Maddy moved into a sitting position on the couch. A toilet break was looming, so the shift was justifiable. "Do I want cheaper phone calls? Absolutely."

"That's good, Mrs O'Doherty, because I have a remarkable deal to share with you. Did you know that you can-"

"Do you want to know why?"

"Excuse me?"

"Do you want to know *why* I want cheaper phone calls?"

The voice, its sun experiencing a partial eclipse, hesitated before responding."I...okay, sure."

Maddy ran a hand across her abdomen. "I want cheaper phone calls because, right now, the phone is just about the only evidence I have that people still exist beyond my couch."

"Oh."

"I'm on something called 'Modified Bed Rest'. I've got to stay on our Navajo three-seater from A Mart as much as is humanly possible. It's so that our little...you don't need to know the details."

"Okay."

"I mean I'm not sick or anything...although my husband is, at this very moment, over at his parents' house informing the whole family that I'm practically at death's door. But that's just to throw them off the scent. So they don't guess I'm...you don't need to know the details."

A shuffling of papers preceded a second hesitation.

"Right...well, I'm pleased you're not...ill. You know our newest offers on overseas and local calls are redefining the industry. The competitors have nothing to compare with our---"

"Do I sound grumpy to you?"

Total eclipse. And perhaps a drop in temperature as well.

"I am grumpy," continued Maddy. "It's not you though. Crazy as it sounds, I don't mind talking to telemarketers these days. It's a distraction. No, I'm grumpy because of other stuff. Being cooped up all day—it's not me. It's not something I ever imagined I would have to do. Scuba diving...riding a motorbike...I had to do those. And I did. I also four-wheel drove the Northern Territory and sailed around the Barrier Reef. You know how many bungy jumps I've had? What's your name?"

"Jared."

"You know how many bungys I've had, Jared? Fourteen! Did three in one day in Queenstown!" Maddy bounced her feet up and down, trying to shake off the pins and needles. "These days I bungy through the TV channels."

"Perhaps I should ring back anoth---"

"But you know what's worse than doing nothing all day, Jared? *The thought that you're still doing too much.* That's the killer. If all this lounging around came with a guarantee of success then I'd be stitching myself to the cushions and singing Hallelujah. But of course, there are no guarantees, are there? So I second-guess every little move I make. Is cooking a meal a stretch? Is a trip to the mailbox courting disaster? Is a pee break going to reveal the latest crushing defeat? It's no way to live, Jared, believe me." Maddy undid the drawstring on her track pants and stood. She took two deep breaths and began the short walk to the bathroom. "But things are going to get better, right? Starting with my phone bills. Tell me, Jared—what can you do for me?"

There was a long pause. Maddy was about to hang up when the reply came:

"I could send you a brochure."

"Thank you, Jared."

Maddy pressed the 'Off' button, crossed her fingers and entered the lavatory.

*

"Hello, Mystery Man of the Backyard."

The trampoline mat beneath Adam's back shifted violently, bouncing his prostrate frame. He sat up and drank before the Sovereign in his right hand could froth over. Michelle laughed then climbed across the springs.

"There's a game of 'Charades' going on inside. What are you hanging around here for like a Nigel?" she asked.

"Just minding my own business."

"Minding your own business."

"Yes."

"Good God! Are you ill?"

Adam watched his sister slip effortlessly into a half-lotus before easing back onto his elbows. "I'm complex," he said.

Michelle nodded. "Yes and I'm big boned." She removed her Pulp slip-on and massaged the toes of her right foot. "We thought you might have snuck off home. To go and tend to that Magic Maddy of yours."

"No, not yet. Soon though."

"Is she alright?"

"She's okay. It's nothing serious."

"Has she been to the doctor?"

"Doesn't want to."

"Oh. Okay." Michelle stole a sip from Adam's beer and removed several strands of grand-dog hair from her shirt. "So…she's definitely not pregnant then."

Adam scoffed, then began a charade. "Two words… sounds like 'vet-trucked'…"

"Answer the question, bro. You and I both know full well that the trampoline was always the keeper of our secrets. I told you about Schoolies here. You told me about getting laid under the Storey Bridge."

"We were kids."

"And now we're having kids?"

Adam looked his sister square in the eye. Make Sure Maddy, standing watch beside the trampoline, deposited a Chinese burn on his forearm. "My wife is not pregnant."

"So you meant what you said before."

"Yes. I meant what I said before." Adam sat up straight, leaned forward. "What about you? Did you mean what you said before?"

"What did I say before?"

"'James and I have discussed it…if our time was in the next year…well that wouldn't be the worst thing in the world…'"

"Did I say that?" Michelle rubbed her forehead and

shrugged. "I don't recall saying that."

Adam gulped down the last of his beer, scrambled to his feet and started jumping. Michelle was caught unawares. Swearing and screaming through several nips from the springs, she untangled her Lotus legs and manoeuvred onto all fours, fists wound tight. The counter-attack was devastating. A stiff arm clotheslined Adam across the left calf at the apex of his jump. The knee to thigh to bum landing saw him rebound sideways and careen off the trampoline amidst a blur of flailing arms and legs. Reg O'Doherty emerged from the barbecue area to discover his eldest daughter examining the condition of her half-exposed backside, his eldest son face down at the foot of the newly-planted lemon tree, and both of them laughing to the point of tears.

"Be careful you two. It's all fun and games until someone loses an eye." He picked up the Sovereign bottle; jettisoned during Adam's ejection and now miraculously standing upright at the entrance to the garden shed. A test swig confirmed the vessel was indeed empty and he strolled back along the paved pathway toward the house. Before passing through the gate he added: "This sort of energy could be used for something much more useful."

"Like becoming a doctor!" shouted Michelle.

"Or writing novels!" chirped Adam.

Reg looked skyward, requested the Almighty give him 'bloody strength' then bolted the gate behind him.

*

Maddy emerged from the lavatory. She turned toward the bathroom entrance, hesitated. The prospect of standing before the long mirror at the wash-basin didn't appeal. Its images weren't welcoming at the best of times; post-cry they required active avoidance.

God, she hated crying. Loathed it. The earnest but dim counsellor she visited after the second miscarriage assessed such enmity to be a scar of childhood bullying. On the surface, it was hard to argue otherwise. The Primary playground taunts had been multi-headed, merciless and often. The 'Howl' nickname had clung to her like a scab, refusing to harden and crumble until the beginning of high school. Maddy, though, felt there was more to the issue than just the cruel classmates of early youth. She sensed something more deep-seated, more visceral. A character flaw? A genetic glitch? A smudge on her soul? Or was she simply a woman very much in touch with her masculine side?

Beyond debate was that crying was more common than laughing these days. More common and all-pervasive. Blubbery episodes tainted the good, sharpened the bad, availed the indifferent a needless gravity. They hovered around the fringes of conversations and ran rampant through the minefields of dreams. They tattooed 'Pathetic!' across your forehead. And if you weren't careful, they would begin to define you.

Maddy peeled away the stray strands of hair plastered against her cheek and returned to the lounge room. At the present moment, progress remained solid. There was still cause to climb on the couch, to seek out the ruts made by her perpetually propped heels. Consequently, the next wave of tears would accompany a sense of relief. For that she could be grateful.

Perhaps even for the rest of the day

*

"So you're going to win our race, hey?"

Adam observed the neighbours' corgi mount a plastic watering can—its fourth inanimate object of affection in the last ten minutes. "What race is that?"

Michelle, heels hooked into the bar at ground level, slid down the mat of the now-tilted trampoline into a squat position just above the springs. She patted her brother's shin. "*The* race. The one about who would live the dream first."

"I don't think it's all over yet."

"Oh, I think it might be. Barring some miracle with the second round of exam results, I've got to wait another year to get into med. And your agent is, in Chris' estimation, a 'bee's boner' away from a big deal. Is that accurate?"

Adam checked his watch. This was dangerous territory. He should've been home by now, and venturing into the writer's realm—a place where time and responsibility fell off the map, a domain in which a bed-resting wife could be forsaken for a national book tour fantasy—had very real implications for his ongoing personal safety. Added to that was the still-present risk of pregnancy disclosure. For all intents and purposes the subject was closed, but it wasn't beyond the former state level Debating representative by his side to have one last salvo left in her armoury.

"Let's say a very well hung bee," he replied. "A porn star bee."

Michelle laughed and plucked a bobble nut off the grass. "That's great, Ad. Really. We're all really proud of you."

"The folks, too, you reckon."

"Of course! Why on earth wouldn't they be?"

Adam waited for a cawing crow in the nearby camphor laurel tree to settle. "I think they'd rather see me stay a teacher. You know, blue chip public servant. Forty hours for forty weeks for forty years. Stability. Security. Superannuation. Worked for them, so why would you want anything different? That's what they're about. Especially Dad."

"I think you're being a bit harsh," contended Michelle, lobbing the nut toward a red, knobbly food ball that Woody thought insulting next to the barbecue and its rissoles from heaven. "They've always been supportive, haven't they?"

"Outwardly, yes."

"Reg even *read* your novel! The last book he read before that was Wally Lewis' biography!"

Adam waved his hands. "I can't fault them for anything they say or do, Shell. But my impression is that, in their heart of hearts, they don't want me to become a writer."

"Bro, they know it's been your dream since grade seven

to write stories. Why wouldn't they want that to come true for you?"

"I think they're afraid."

"Of what? That you won't be able to provide for their grandkids?"

Adam glanced left then right. Make Sure Maddy was nowhere to be seen. He wasn't buying it. She was probably tucked in behind the tilted tramp, baseball bat in hand.

"*I think they're afraid I won't provide grandkids,* Shell. I think they imagine there's no place for kids in a writer's life."

"Well, you don't believe that yourself, do you."

"No."

"So later on when you've got the kids and the career, when you've turned your dream into a cashed-up, successful reality and they're out showing their baby spew medals of honour, they'll realise that you, like Oprah and Brad and Ange and James Packer and Maxine McKew and Microsoft and most of the supermodels, can truly, ruly have it all." Michelle grabbed her brother's hand, raised it to the sky and launched into a tone deaf Freddie Mercury impression: "You are a champion…YOU are a champion…no time for teaching…'cos you are a champion…."

The corgi next door howled his approval, prompting guttural rebukes from both male and female voices within the house. The contrary pooch waddled over to an abandoned tricycle.

"Too bad he can't fulfil the folks' wishes," conceded Shell, noting the corgi's customary interaction. She shouted in the direction of the barbecue area—"James, honey! I've been inspired! Take me home, darling!"—then clapped her hands.

As she ducked her head under the outer wire of the clothesline, Adam called after her:

"I want to tell you something…before you go."

"What?"

"Something you should know."

He motioned for her to rejoin him at the trampoline.

When she arrived, he cupped his hands around her ear.

"We're both going to win the race," he whispered.

The two eldest children of Reginald and Eileen O'Doherty embraced then sprinted for the glory of being first to release the bolted back gate.

*

Maddy accepted the glass of water offered by her husband then thumbed the stereo remote. Diana Ah Naid's 'I Go Off' leapt out of the speakers.

"So they believed I was sick."

"Yes."

"What did you say I had?"

"Hypochondria."

Maddy took a sip and nodded. "Good choice." She observed a gecko scuttle across the far cornice of the living room. "Was the pressure on?"

"No more than usual."

"Really? With the birthday and everything?"

Adam laid a basket of wrinkled clothes at the foot of the ironing board and scrutinised the appliance for an 'On' switch. "Alright, maybe a bit more than usual. I was asked twice if you were pregnant."

"Hey?"

"I was asked twice if you were-"

"You mean directly?"

"Yes."

"'Is Maddy pregnant?'"

"Michelle's words exactly. Kel spoke in 'Kellinese', but the implication was the same."

"And you gave nothing away, fella?"

"Nothing."

"No hints?"

"Nada."

Maddy dabbed some water on her forehead and neck. "But you wanted to tell, didn't you."

"With every fibre of my being."

"Well then how did you avoid giving it away?"

"Easy," replied Adam, temporarily abandoning his ironing post for a position beside the couch. The opening 'two-knee kneel' of the new week ensued. "I had you there."

"What, my evil twin?"

"Something like that."

The stereo hummed and whirred as the shuffle command scoured the CDs for its next song—Alex Lloyd's 'Black the Sun'. Adam kissed Maddy on both eyes, shook hands with Make Sure Maddy (she was semi-conscious and stretched out in the recliner) and returned to his final chore of the evening. 'Black the Sun' ambled through the room's recesses then gave way to the still life echoes of Massive Attack's 'Teardrop'.

"Thank you, gorgeous handsome man."

"I wouldn't be too hasty," replied Adam, examining the crease that had materialised in a pair of 501's.

Maddy smiled. She lifted her shirt, exposing her midriff. "You know what, Kiddo? I think you should be the solution to this 'tell or not to tell' situation. Next time you're around Daddy's family, try to reveal yourself to them. Sing. Shout out to them. Communicate with morse code. Anything short of a John Hurt, Alien-type excursion through Mummy's sternum."

She cupped her ear with her right hand, her navel with the left.

"Any suggestions from you, Dad?"

*

Adam yawned as he sat down at the computer.

I really should be in bed, he thought.

The seven hours of night-time remaining promised disturbance. Maddy was dead to the world right now; later she would toss and turn like a leaf in a September westerly. She would grind her teeth. She would yell things in her sleep.

She might cry. In the waking hours, and on the short drive to Dawn Marks' home clinic for the check-up, her worst imaginings would've dulled. But there would be nothing approaching optimism. The best that could be hoped for was relief, and that would only arrive in the late afternoon, after every last suspicion had been rounded up and arrested.

Adam scrolled down 'The Umbilical Word'. He was surprised to find the correspondence now stretched to twenty pages. *The Ordinary Man's Enemy* had never moved as quickly as this. At the bottom was a cut-and-pasted reply to his most recent entry. He smiled, pulled his shoulders back and edged the ergonomic chair closer to the desk.

"Purge, Mad," he whispered. "You're in good hands."

*

From: "Tin Lid" <womb@almighty.com>
To: "Adam O'Doherty" <edam_odoh@fathertobe.com>
Subject: RE:Blab

Dad

How come you're not supposed to tell anyone about me?

I asked The Chief if it was one of those 'vow of silence' things. **Sort of** was the reply. Whatever!

Can you be a bit more helpful?

B

5

From: "Adam O'Doherty" <edam_odoh@fathertobe.com>
To: "Tin Lid" <womb@almighty.com>
Subject: Wanted

B

Why are we not supposed to tell people about you yet? Good question. Not the standard child-to-father poser like 'Why is the sky blue?' or 'Why isn't there a black Wiggle' or 'Why are you lying on top of Mummy like that?' At the outset, let me make this clear—we're certainly not ashamed of you or embarrassed by your presence on the scene. You are not an accident. You are not the product of a night on the booze or a forgotten pill or an inadequate piece of latex (mark down these concepts in your 2020 diary). You are very, VERY much planned and very, VERY much wanted. And, in a sense, that's the reason why Mum is *not* the word. Your mother won't hear of any 'baby discussion' until the first twelve weeks has been safely negotiated. Were it possible, I believe she would delay acknowledgement of the pregnancy until you were physically in her arms.

This is not to say there is no voice at all in her. Without the plague of the past—'History' as we refer to it—she would be shouting your name from the rooftops. Silence, though, is safer, without additional complication. No one on this earth could begrudge your mother silence, B, least of all myself....

*

Dawn Marks removed the fetal heart monitor from Maddy's girth and laughed.

"You really should stay off the Horlicks!"

Maddy pulled her shirt down and lifted her knees. The examination table holding her weight gave a tiny creak. "It's not good, is it?"

The midwife placed her diary on an ornate wall-shelf stacked with birthing brochures. She returned to the table, took up Maddy's hand, gave it a pat.

"Sometimes they do aerobics and sometimes they watch TV."

"Not throwing up isn't good at this stage either. And that's happened…hasn't it, Adam. Adam?"

He was reading a recent addition to the clinic corkboard – a quote from the ancient Greek physician, Soranus, addressing the question 'What persons are fit to become midwives?':

"… A suitable person will be literate, with her wits about her, possessed of a good memory, loving work, respectable and not unduly handicapped as regards her senses, sound of limb, robust, and, according to some people endowed with long slim fingers and short nails at her fingertips."

Nothing about an 'All Blacks Forever' tattoo on the shoulder blade. Or sequinned Doc Martens on the feet. Or a pair of quick-blinking, goggly eyes. Adam was not at all surprised at Maddy's admission of finding comfort in those eyes. Eyes like that, she argued, wouldn't miss a thing.

"I'm sure everything's okay, Mad."

"The key thing right now is size and heartbeat," assured Dawn. "And your little poppet gets a big tick in both boxes."

Maddy took a deep breath and studied the print of Van Gogh's 'Irises' on the opposite wall. "So you don't think I'm doing too much then."

"You're being very good."

"I could try to do less. Maybe I could hang on a little longer before going to the toilet. And Adam could try and do all my meals the night before. Right, fella?"

"Yeah." Adam moved toward his wife, fortifying the shaky conviction in his voice along the way. "Yes, yes, I could. I probably should be doing that already."

Dawn smiled. She extended her arms and drew the couple into a tight, slightly bent over scrum. "Listen, you guys. I'm not surprised to hear you saying these things. Given what's happened to you in the past...you've got every right to feel... well, concerned. But let me tell you this—you don't have to feel guilty about what you're doing or not doing. Really. From what you've told me, it's clear to me you're both doing a wonderful job. And the proof's in the results today."

The midwife released the huddle, plucked a stamp off the shelf and deposited a smiley-face on the right hand of both patient and partner.

"Find something else to feel guilty about!"

*

Adam licked his thumb and rubbed away at the stamp. The smiley-face, now four days old, remained smearless, smudgeless, assuredly uncorrupted.

"I'll fix you later, you little bastard," he mumbled. "I've got sandpaper in my desk."

He hid the offending hand under the staffroom table, bowed his head and tried, for the hundredth time in the last five minutes, to swallow the large, free-range, grain-fed, prime-cut fillet of guilt lodged in his throat. All around him, Carsmair colleagues sought to prolong the struggle by patting him on the back.

They were to blame:

"So is Elizabeth Hurley the new Blessed Virgin or something?"

"Breast feeding over formula? Huh! Wait till they get teeth!"

"Dressing a small child is like stuffing an octopus inside a string bag...agree?"What manner of pre-bell, morning bloody coffee talk was that? It was an ambush, no less. No "Did you see those anti-war rallies?', or 'What a great episode of 'The Bill' last night!', or 'How come the selectors don't like Steve Waugh any more?'. None of that harmless fare. Just...unmentionables. Consequently, what recourse could a man in the line of fire have but to abandon his mischievous, perhaps malicious peers, walk to the staff whiteboard, pick up a pen, and write 'MADDY'S PREGNANT!' in bold green, non-permanent strokes? They were responsible. Them and Make Sure Maddy. Stress leave or no stress leave, she should have been on hand.

The problem now was damage control. Work had suffered a core meltdown and leaks required containment. Verbal congratulations could be kept within house. The inevitable card and flowers could be stashed away in the garage. Second-hand baby items would be stockpiled in the car boot until-

"Well, we *certainly* have something to talk about this evening, don't we?"

Adam lifted his head off the table. Halfway toward registering Jenna's flushed and frantic features, he reconnected with the awful truth:

Dinner.

The Grimsons.

Their place.

With Maddy.

TONIGHT!

"I think I have to go ring your lovely wife right this very minute!"

Adam clutched his friend's blouse before a single departing stride was complete. "Don't...please don't."

"Why on Earth not?"

"It's...it's supposed to be a secret. Maddy doesn't want people to know right now. It's important to her that people don't know right now."

"Well then why the hell did you just make a neon sign out of it?"

"I couldn't help it! The whole table was going on about babies. And Make Sure Maddy wasn't keeping me in line."

"Make...Sure...Maddy?"

"And, really, isn't getting a pregnancy out in the open better anyway? Creates positive, healthy energy and all that?"

Jenna lifted Adam's hand from her elbow and eased it onto the table. She sat in the nearest chair and stroked the appendage like it was a flighty pet.

"You told because you're an idiot, didn't you?"

"Positive energy, Jay-"

"Didn't you?"

"Yes, I'm an idiot."

Jenna surveyed the room. The buzz surged with each new arrival, each new insider on the scene. "You'd better tell everyone."

Adam shook his head. "Not necessary. Only one person needs to know. One person at risk of blowing everything wide open."

Jenna surveyed the room a second time. Unsure of the designated target, she looked back toward Adam. He did a double-take.

"Me?"

"You, Sweetheart."

"Me!"

"You!"

"You think I'm the risk?"

"You're the only one who talks about their personal hygiene on a regular basis."

"That's just making conversation."

"You're the only one who would go and ring Maddy this instant. And you're the only one we're having dinner with tonight."

"What about Boyd?"

"I think he can keep a secret."

"So can I!"

"Are you sure?"

Jenna folded her arms and tilted her head side to side, stretching her neck. "Quite the irony, Mr Writer. *You* casting aspersions on *my* ability to keep a secret."

Adam released the handshake of the morning cleaner—"Knocked one through the covers, ay? On ya, son..."—and knelt, single knee, beside his closest teaching buddy.

"Jay, I'm sorry. You're spot on—I have no right to be hassling you given my stuff-up. Forgive me. I know you'll stay *mum* tonight."

Jenna held out for a brief moment, smiled, then ended the sad grovel with an 'Eat carpet!' shove.

*

From: "Tin Lid" <womb@almighty.com>
To: "Adam O'Doherty" <edam_odoh@fathertobe.com>
Subject: It's Okay

Hey Dad, I'm hoping you get this message before you visit the Grimsons this eve.

Don't worry about your 'stuff-up'. I'm stoked there are more people who know I'm around.

Maybe you should pull Mum aside before you leave, let her know you let it slip to your friends. You gave the silent thing a shot, but when something is very, VERY much planned and very, VERY much wanted it's hard to be patient, yeah?

I think she'll totally understand.

*

Adam closed the file and pincer-gripped the bridge of his nose.

"I think she'll have my guts for garters, B," he murmured.

*

The front door of 'Coola Vista's apartment number 10 opened before the doorbell had completed its third chime.

"Hi! How are you? Come in, come in!"

"Wow!" exclaimed Maddy. "Greeted by *both* hosts. Now there's hospitality, hey Adam?"

Adam glared at each host in turn. "Emphasis on the 'hospital'."

"Sit down on the couch, groovers, and Boyd will get us some drinks. What would you like Maddy? Wine? Bacardi Breezer?"

"Just water would be fine, Jen."

"Wise choice—you haven't been feeling the best lately,

have you. Tummy bug and such. For you, Ad?"

"Double scotch on the rocks."

"Mmm...yes, that sounds delish. I'll have one of those as well, Boyd, my darling."

"Jenna, you should probably slow down for a bit."

Jenna waved airily in the direction of the kitchen, then flopped down onto the couch, between the O'Dohertys.

"So," she said clamping a hand on each adjacent thigh, "How's the weather?"

"Stable," hinted Adam. "For the moment."

"John Schluter reckoned there would be a storm tonight," added Maddy.

"Really?"

"Could be a strong one, he said."

"Ah, but they get it wrong so often don't they? John Schlooper and the rest of these guys probably don't know anything at all. And they should admit it! Like me! I don't know anything at all! Not a thing!"

"About the weather?" enquired Adam.

"About *anything*! I don't know anything about anything, guys. I have no knowledge of any matter that might be of any consequence. To anything."

Boyd emerged from the kitchen and distributed the drinks. Jenna lifted her scotch (and soda) skyward, splashing the curtains in the process.

"A toast...to nothing in particular!"

*

From: "Adam O'Doherty" <edam_odoh@fathertobe.com>
To: "Tin Lid" <womb@almighty.com>
Subject: Insert swear word here...

...It got worse.

By the end of the first hour, she was responding to everything Maddy said with a tilt of the head and a saccharine-laced 'ohhhh'. Stolen glances in the direction of Maddy's mid-section became lingering looks, then outright ogles. To ward off suspicion, Boyd would prise the glass from her hand, take her by the elbow and guide her into the kitchen under the pretext of 'checking the chook' (I think our Chicken Tikka Masala had higher viewer ratings than 'The Bachelorette'). The one occasion babies/births/related topics were overtly raised—for Almighty knows what reason, B, your mother felt compelled to discuss the deadly protective instincts of the female hippopotamus—Jay-Jay downed her after-dinner glass of port in one swig, then disappeared to the toilet for ten minutes.

It was tantamount to torture. And in the interests of saving my teaching colleague from a rubber room, I intended to end the suffering and make it an early night.

Early night?

Yes.

An end to the suffering?

No %#$@* chance...

*

BAP BAP BAP BAP

Adam ceased dealing the 'Luxor Hotel' deck of cards in his hands. He glared at Boyd.

"That wasn't thunder was it."

"No."

"That was the door."

The concerned host shrugged and nodded. Adam directed an accusing eye toward Jenna.

"Probably Jehovah's Witneshesh," she replied, several cards falling from her grasp as she crossed her heart. "This shtorm's gunna be the end of the world!"

Boyd opened the door. Carsmair State High's three student teachers crossed the threshold. Glittery bowler hats were perched on their heads. Nasally party-favours lunged back and forth from their lips. A homemade banner that read 'GREAT STUFF...YOU'RE UP THE DUFF!!!' extended the length of their accumulated hipster belt-lines. A dazed Jenna wandered in and around the team, looking them up and down, inspecting them like a shell-shocked drill sergeant.

"Lisha, weren't you guysh going to Café Neon tonight?"

Lisa threw a streamer to indicate the affirmative.

"This ishn't Café Neon, darling!"

Lisa craned her neck. "Where's your wife, Adam?"

Adam pointed a limp finger in the direction of the bathroom then continued flicking cards at the slowly rotating ceiling fan. Electrical disturbance prompted the corner lamp to wink. Jenna cradled Lisa's face in her hands.

"Why are you here?"

"You said, 'Have a drink with us this evening'."

"For ush! *For* ush!" Jenna lurched toward the table, palms pressed together. "I shaid 'for ush', Adam! I shwear!"

Adam extracted the 'Joker' from the remaining deck and slapped it against his forehead.

"I'm sorry, there's been a mistake. You have to go, girls," said Boyd, attempting to herd the gate crashing trio toward the exit. "Here's a brolly and some money for a cab. There's a rank just outside the-"

"Should I have brought two Vienettas for dessert?"

Five pairs of eyes crowded the surprise party's latecomer. Maddy preferred to focus on Adam. He lay face down on the table, surrounded by clubs and spades. Outside, the heavens gave way. Horizontal waves of rain rattled the louver window frames.

Jenna plucked the party favour from Lisa's mouth and sat down in the chair next to Adam.

"Shecret's out I guess, Ad. Time for the truth."

She took up the nearest alcoholic vessel—Boyd's half-full Ruski—and patted her stomach.

"I'm with child," she said and downed the remaining vodka mix. "To my hushband," she added.

The pendulum of attention now swung toward the host. The student teachers handed their cab money back. Maddy stood slightly hunched, leaning to the left, face puckered with serious intent. Were the truth to be hiding behind Boyd, she would not let the former footballer's ample frame provide indefinite asylum. Adam lifted his head from the table, mouth agape, eyes blinking. Was I just struck by lightning? he thought.

Boyd scanned each of his observers then gave an exaggerated wipe of his forehead.

"Thank Christ for that, hey?" he said. "Now Jen and I can stop pretending."

He peeled the Joker off Adam's brow and headed for the toilet. He would not be seen for ten minutes.

*

From: "Adam O'Doherty" <edam_odoh@fathertobe.com>
To: "Tin Lid" <womb@almighty.com>
Subject: Insert swear word here...

...Mercifully, follow-up interrogation of the Grimsons was thwarted—the thunderstorm (thank your boss for me) brought an abrupt end to the power supply and the proceedings. Just prior to leaving, I cornered Boyd while he was on hold with Energex...

*

"You reckon Jay-Jay's little stunt worked?"

"Only if Maddy is taking hallucinogens."

"How are you going to get out of it?"

"Fess up."

"That might not be advisable at this point in time."

Boyd nodded. "Alright, Jen and I had better make the most of this blackout then."

*

From: "Adam O'Doherty" <edam_odoh@fathertobe.com>
To: "Tin Lid" <womb@almighty.com>
Subject: Insert swear word here...

...I really don't know whether Mum bought any of it, B. She offered her congratulations to the 'lucky' couple (likewise three sheepish student teachers), but didn't explore further. And on the way home she seemed to bounce between acceptance –

"We'll have to buy them a gift..."

– and incredulity:

"She drank an awful lot for someone who is pregnant."

Fooled? Not fooled? No idea.

Out of all this mess, though, some positive news: Mum has decided to finally tell! She informed me twenty minutes ago, just before going to bed. And while it's unlikely to involve booze, banners and bald-faced lies, it will be soon. Sunday to be precise, at the folks' place.

You little %#$@* beauty.

6

Maddy wriggled into a more comfy couch groove then held her hands up, thumb to fingers, in front of her face. The right was gloved in a navy blue Holeproof quarter sock, the left wore a Razzamatazz knee-high. She eyeballed each puppet before commencing:

"Reg and Eileen—there's something we should... hmmm...Adam and I have something to say...no no...Guess what? We've got the very thing you've been waiting for!... Eurgh! Okay—Adam and I are expecting our first baby...as distinct from our twenty-first."

She giggled and engaged the ceiling she now knew like an old school friend. Reg and Eileen, despite the absence of any sewn on button eyes, stared at each other then back at their daughter-in-law.

"Well at least I won't be saying I am 'with child'!"

Maddy peeled off the puppets and wound them into a single ball. She tossed it at the potted aloe vera plant acting as a stop for the French doors. The muted television countered the harsh dismissal with Ricki Lake's bold, bouncing by-line of the day: *'Yo Girlfriend! Get wit your parents-in-law and get some RESPECT!'*

"I could always leave it up to Daddy, Kiddo," she said, massaging her abdomen. "He's been itching to tell since we found out about you. And they are *his* parents after all. I'm sure he will find the right words for the occasion."

*

"I have no absolutely no idea what to say."

Dilip applauded the final finisher's touch in the Under 15 Boys' backstroke then flipped up the sunglasses attachment of his spectacles.

"A writer without words—that is, indeed, a crisis."

"I need help."

"Perhaps you should request our Ms Grimson's presence at the gathering."

Adam, hand held over his forehead to shield the February glare, scanned the terraces for his saviour. He found her standing at the head of the Cosgrove cheer squad, hips waggling, pom-poms flailing, in full voice with what Adam estimated to be her four-hundredth war cry of the Carsmair inter-house swimming carnival.

"A woman in such a delicate condition—I don't think I want to trouble her a second time."

"Of course."

Adam pulled his borrowed Akubra lower. "God, I hate these sports days. When's this supposed to finish?"

"In about fifteen minutes," replied Dilip, checking his watch. "The teachers' relay is the final event."

"The 'Cardiac Crawl', hey? Is The Sarge going round again?"

"Oh yes. He is such a fit fellow for his age. There's a rumour circulating that he's staying in shape in case they bring back conscription."

"Wouldn't put it past this PM."

"And did you know Cal's swimming this year, too?"

"You're joking."

"It's true, my friend. First time in twenty years apparently. He broke the news at lunchtime. He claimed he was going to dive in and stay there. Said his daughter was driving him to it."

"She still going through with the wedding to the internet guy then?"

Dilip assured a nearby student that the school swimming carnival was not an appropriate forum for the discussion of breasts as floatation aids then shook his head. "The engagement's off. According to Cal, the marriage would've interfered with her new career as a pole dancer."

"Is that right?"

The gun fired, commanding the final bank of student competitors to forget about the early bus and have one last thrash in the water / chlorine / unidentifiables' mix. An announcement followed over the PA:

"Would all the brave teachers involved in the staff relay make your way down to the marshalling area, please.."

Whoops and whistles echoed across the grandstands. Jokes about gut sizes and sock tans and questionable swimming pedigrees meandered through a sardined, sunburnt student population. The non-participating staff, hamstrung by their own similar but unpublicised jibes, feigned ignorance.

"Dee, I don't even know *how* I'm going to tell Mum and Dad, let alone what I'll tell them," declared Adam. "They've been wanting this for so long...I'm afraid they'll have a stroke if I tell them point blank!"

Dilip gave a wave of encouragement to the History department squad. "Perhaps it would be wisest to let them be your cue."

"How so?"

"You have said they are always asking when you are going to give them a grandchild. This time around you will have the perfect answer!"

"It's that easy, is it?"

"We have a saying in India: 'There is nothing more obvious than the sunlight upon your face'."

Adam crinkled his nose. "I still think they might keel over."

"My friend, don't underestimate the resiliency of parents. Having children shows you how to take one on the chin and stay standing. You become Muhammad Ali!"

The teachers moved onto the blocks. Callum Morecroft, wearing an aged pair of purple Speedos, responded to the call of 'Take your mark' by placing his hands on his hips.

BANG!

The veteran of Carsmair belly-flopped into the water and slipped from sight. After several seconds, the ripples began to smooth. The lane ropes' bounce became a diminishing tremor. Colleagues in the adjoining lanes heaved and cleaved through the wash, unprepared to go back to assist, perhaps fearful that if they stopped they too might end up on the bottom of the pool.

The concerned crowd shifted to the edge of their seats. The designated lifesaver—Mr Barton, a junior manual arts teacher—fidgeted, attempting to recall his first aid ABC. Then, just when it seemed to Adam that the early bus might require a siren and flashing lights, Cal Morecroft surfaced and commenced a slow but purposeful sidestroke that would carry him the required distance.

"You become Ian Thorpe, too, I guess," remarked Dilip.

*

From: "Adam O'Doherty" <edam_odoh@fathertobe.com>
To: "Tin Lid" <womb@almighty.com>
Subject: Coming Out Day (figuratively speaking)

Well, we've figured out the particulars for the grandparent scoop tomorrow, except for *where* it might take place. Here are the prices:

evens—the bar

3/1—the barbecue

4/1—the other barbecue

5/1—adjacent to Woody's food bowl

8/1—the new caravan we must inspect every time we go over there

10/1—underneath the poster of the 1987 Queensland State of Origin team

20/1—the spa

100/1—the trampoline

One more sleep, B. I truly believe revealing you to the world at last will be good for all concerned.

*

From: "Tin Lid" <womb@almighty.com>
To: "Adam O'Doherty" <edam_odoh@fathertobe.com>
Subject: RE: Coming Out Day (figuratively speaking)

I'll make sure I wear my best suit.

*

Adam watched his father ease the 'Wally Lewis Testimonial' port from the display shelf and place it on the bar. It was the third public appearance of the venerated Immortal's vintage in the last five years—the previous occasions being last year's unexpected blow-in from a distant Irish cousin and the Y2K 'New Year's Rockin' Eve'.

"Did you say *you've* got great news, Dad?"

Reg blew the dust off the crafted wooden box and wiped the branded image of the King's face with a damp Chux. "Not me pur-say. Michelle."

"Shelley?"

"She's got news good enough for ten Big Pineapple pictures, I kid you not!"

"That's pretty good."

"Bloody oath."

"What's, um...what's it about?"

"Nah-ah. She's going to ring later to tell you and Madeline in person. Until then, my lips are---" he trowelled his mouth, "---Spakfilla."

Adam bit his bottom lip and looked around. "You're certainly pumped up about this."

"I'm fit to burst, son! Might have to have an extra one of Doctor Long's blood pressure pills before the day's out!"

"No doubt."

As Reg exited to rejoin the game of 'Balderdash' taking place on the back deck, Adam noted O'Doherty Senior's choice of perambulation: a half-shuffle, half-jog with a heel click thrown in for good measure.

"Stay on the blocks for a little while longer, Thorpey," he muttered, replacing the palm cards in his top pocket.

*

"She's pregnant!"

Adam stared at his ebullient wife with a mixture of incredulity and shock.

"Pardon?"

"Your sister's pregnant, Adam! It's obvious!"

"Shell's been accepted into Medicine, Mad. She's not pregnant."

"She is!"

"She isn't!"

"She *is*!"

"Babe, they weren't even trying!"

"You said they'd discussed it."

"Yes, I did. And one thing I've learned in the past six years is that it takes a lot more than just discussion to make a baby. If it took discussion alone, we'd have enough kids to make the Hilton our family home."

"You also told me she said there was 'no right time', and that their 'time' could be within the year. She said that, didn't she?"

"Yeah."

"Their time might be now!"

"It wouldn't happen this quick, surely."

"Adam, not everyone has to go through what we've experienced."

Adam stretched his arms toward the beam above—the same structure supporting the foot of the suspended hammock at his midriff. He then resumed his consideration of Maddy, semi-reclined, left leg flopped over the side, swinging gently in the nylon weave. She had a case. Grandchildren, and the lack thereof, had inexplicably vanished from the conversational radar today. Plenty of talk about Uncle Trev's motorised cart exploits, and whether the government had made Australia more of a target for terrorism, and the sights, sounds and, yes, smells of the caravan sales yards. Reg had even dusted off a long forgotten heirloom—the story of how he lost his sunglasses kissing the Blarney Stone. But concerning the next generation of O'Dohertys? Not a peep from either parent. And that was a continental shift to shake the very axis of the world.

There had to be some sort of logical explanation, enrolment in 'Desperate Oldies Anonymous' or the like.

"It makes sense, doesn't it?" said Maddy, correctly appraising her husband's faraway look and drumming fingers.

Adam gave a non-committal shrug. "I just hope it's, you know, getting into Med."

"You 'hope' for that? Why would you 'hope' for that? Are you against having a little niece or nephew?"

"Of course not."

"Is this a sibling rivalry thing?"

"Jesus, Maddy. Give me a little bit of credit."

"So why 'hope' it's not a pregnancy? It's all rather…oh. Oh-oh-oh." Maddy clicked her fingers. "Medicine is *something she's had to work for*. It's something that didn't come easy."

"It's her dream."

"And she's earned it…right?"

"Bloody oath."

"And that's the way it should be with dreams?"

"Well, I would have loved my first two stories being published and hitting the big time…but, yeah, I guess if it comes too easy you don't appreciate it enough."

"Hence, you would prefer it if she wasn't pregnant. She hasn't paid her dues on that one yet."

Adam brought his hands down from the overhead beam and stilled the hammock. He lowered both knees onto the polished hardwood deck.

"Wouldn't it upset you if it happened just like that? I mean, when you worked on the phones at Centrelink…those teenage mums…."

His voice trailed away. Those teenage mums. Those gum-chewing, talking-on-the-mobile, sometimes swearing, always deflating, callow, constant teenage mums. They hadn't even appreciated the government handouts, let alone the lives so easily and immediately brought into being within them. Michelle O'Doherty was a world apart from those teenage mums and Maddy told him so.

"I don't know," conceded Adam, "Maybe it's neither of these things. Maybe they bought another grand-dog."

"Guys!"

The couple paused. Eileen stood at the threshold of the deck, eyes dancing behind her half-moon reading glasses, right fist raised to her ear.

"Phone!"

*

From: "Adam O'Doherty" <edam_odoh@fathertobe.com>
To: "Tin Lid" <womb@almighty.com>
Subject: The best laid plans...

I brought 'The Umbilical Word' on disk with me and have snuck away to the folks' state-of-the-art, Pentium 4, two thousand dollar 'Hearts' game to bring you this update.

If you haven't already worked out the goings-on of the last hour, little B, if the shouting and the cork-popping and the crying and the continuous loop of Guns 'n Roses hasn't afforded you enough clues, then here's a brief summary of this afternoon's events:

Michelle rings about one o'clock...

*

"Hello?"

"Brud! It's Shell. How goes it?"

"Fine. How goes it with you?"

"Not sure. I'm totally overwhelmed at the moment."

Adam observed the expectant crew standing by. Maddy and Eileen were seated on the sofa, unblinking, arms linked. Chris commenced an index finger drum roll on the adjacent bar stool. Woody lay on the terracotta tile floor, ears pricked for the first signs of release from the wound-up energy surrounding. Reg was inexplicably absent, yet his presence remained keen, courtesy of the moment's musical score: Herb Alpert's 'Tijuana Taxi'.

"Overwhelmed, Shell? I would've thought something like 'blessed' or 'lucky bastard'."

A pause. "Do…you know?"

Adam attempted to smooth a folded pocket on his cargo shorts. "Pretty much."

A squeal plumed out of the receiver. "Can you believe it! God, I can't! I was convinced I'd have to wait, you know? I was sure it wouldn't happen right now, but…God! No doubt it's going to be hard work, but it'll be a labour of love, hey? Sorry about the bad pun. God! Babies…motherhood is such a precious gift, Ad!"

*

From: "Adam O'Doherty" <edam_odoh@fathertobe.com>
To: "Tin Lid" <womb@almighty.com>
Subject: The best laid plans…

…her voice has an almost helium quality about it and her machine gun sentences fire off round after round of incredulity. I must confess—I'm annoyed. She doesn't know the first thing about waiting. She doesn't know the first thing about any of this! She never had her body betray her in unfathomable ways. She never got down on her knees and prayed with white-knuckled, shaking hands. She never cursed The Almighty with every epithet known to woman. She never had a husband writing lists of reasons why she wasn't a failure. She never endured anything remotely resembling History. 'Motherhood is precious'—my sister has no concept, no clue. And as far as a 'gift' is concerned, not everyone gets it for nothing…

*

"Yeah, that's great. Super. So, when do you deliver?"

"Sorry?"

"When will you be bringing a new life into the world?"

Michelle mumbles some calculations then laughs. "Probably not for a good ten years."

"Yeah, that's super…hey?"

"Not until I'm qualified."

"What!"

"I could probably assist on a few before then."

"Assist…assist…because you got into…and obstetrics is…"

"Why are you so interested in the delivery stuff? Is your Magic Maddy pregnant after all? Brud?"

Adam looked again to the nervous spectators and discovered Reg returning to the fold. He was wearing a surgical mask.

"Adam?"

*

From: "Adam O'Doherty" <edam_odoh@fathertobe.com>
To: "Tin Lid" <womb@almighty.com>
Subject: The best laid plans…

…I remove my palm from the receiver and hold the phone at arm's length, out in front of my face…

*

"Mum, Dad, Shelley, anybody else who cares to know… Maddy's pregnant. We're going to have a baby."

*

From: "Adam O'Doherty" <edam_odoh@fathertobe.com>
To: "Tin Lid" <womb@almighty.com>
Subject: The best laid plans…

…That was at twenty-past one. With the exception of a hyperventilating Reg requiring a paper bag and Chris' selection of 'Sweet Child Of Mine' as the celebratory tune, the ensuing forty minutes has been all good.

I'm exhausted, a little light-headed from the champagne, but happy. You're thirteen weeks old, B. Your presence has been acknowledged.

Your coming is assured. All is healthy in our world and this is just the beginning.

Talk to you soon.

love Dad

p.s. Listen up for a phone call to Canada! I don't think Maddy can wait any longer than twelve hours to ring them!

*

From: "Tin Lid" <womb@almighty.com>
To: "Adam O'Doherty" <edam_odoh@fathertobe.com>
Subject: Re: The best laid plans...

Yeah, Mum can't wait alright. She's rung her fam a lot since you went back to school. So much in fact that the big news won't be much of a surprise. The Top Toga here says **the constant contact had them thinking there was either a divorce or a pregnancy in the wind.** Apparently, they've now ruled out the first...although that might change with the next phone bill, hey?

Hope you're not too bummed. Mum promised me she'd lay off the hot salsa bean dip if I kept it all hush-hush.

Any of that champagne left?

Doctors, Dragons and Dougie Defiance

7

From: "Adam O'Doherty" <edam_odoh@fathertobe.com>
To: "Tin Lid" <womb@almighty.com>
Subject: The Public Eye

When you turn eighteen and are legally permitted to wet the neck a few times, drink champagne by all means, but stay right away from Reginald Harris O'Doherty's 'Bitter Reg' home-brewed beer. Grandad's grog has a number of nasty day-after side effects: hairy tongue, burning throat, curious buzzing in the left ear. A second drink of the stuff produces much worse. Did you hear him offer Mum a glass? She declined. Said she'd like to remain conscious for remainder of the pregnancy.

Not surprising then that after six or so BRs school has been something of a haze so far today. It didn't stop me telling about the *telling* at lunchtime. 'Dad-to-be' Boyd couldn't contain his delight.

*

"Thank Christ for that! It's like I've had to wear this really ugly tie for the last few days and…oh, sorry. Hey, it looks really good on you though, O'Doherty. Doesn't it, Jen?"

Jenna Grimson, chewing the plastic lid of a ball-point in preference to her Caesar salad lunch, shook her head and spoke out of the side of her mouth.

"How am I going to tell Maddy I'm not…you know…like you guys, like her? It's so embarrassing."

Adam laid a hand on his friend's arm. "With everything out in the open she really won't mind. She'll understand the intent behind the fib."

"Do you know where I can get my hands on one of those fake bellies?"

"Sweetheart, Maddy *really* won't mind and she'll *understand* the intent behind the fib."

Jenna bounced an index finger along the student teachers' revised banner—'WONDERFUL NEWS…WE HAD NO CLUES!!!'—presented to Adam before first bell and now laid out on the lunch table. She gave the gnarled plastic cap to her husband and put her face in her hands.

"I just gotta find the right moment," she mumbled.

"Please find it soon, precious," pleaded Boyd.

Adam smiled and commenced rolling the banner into a cylinder.

*

Maddy smiled at the pleasant, perspiring Mormon pair standing at the threshold of the front door. In the missionaries' hands were fans of brochures—'The Nature of God', 'The Purpose of Life', 'The Importance of Family', 'Together Forever'….

"Oscar, Delroy, all I can say is it's a shame."

The Mormons glanced sideways at each other. Responses like this carried weight. They could be the preface to an attack—verbal, physical, canine or otherwise. Sure, this woman seemed friendly enough, indeed appeared quite receptive to all the many bounties offered by the Heavenly Father. But more than one experience had shown 'friendly and receptive' to be concealing a mean streak and an even meaner rottweiler.

"It is a shame," continued Maddy, "because you should've been here last week. I would've given you an ear. Hell, you might've even converted me! You see I'm on Modified Bed Rest. I'm on it because we're trying to ensure…you don't need to know the details. But anyway, last week was pretty hard. I felt like I was…" she noted the missionaries' stack hats, "…riding up a steep hill in the wrong gear."

Oscar, Caucasian and wiry, cocked his head to the left, indicating his gilt-edged empathy for hardships on the two-wheeled climb of life. Delroy, African-American and muscular, cocked his head to the right, primed for any sudden onrush of a crazed, collared, carnivorous Satan.

"But now, I'm feeling a lot better. I feel like things are finally moving in the right direction. Okay, there's still a long way to go to get to the top of the hill, but at least I'm in the right gear now." Maddy began drawing brochures out of the missionaries' grasp. "I'm still desperately short of reading material, though. Aren't I, Kiddo?"

The Mormons flinched.

"Keed-o," offered Oscar. "Would that happen to be the name of your-"

Delroy was taking no chances. He spun his partner around, hustled him down the stairs and lifted him onto his bike. Observing their urgent retreat down the driveway, Maddy called out through cupped hands:

"'Kiddo' isn't a dog! It's just what I call our…you don't need to know the details!"

After a goodbye wave, she closed the front door and brought her new literature to the coffee table.

"'*The answers to all of life's important questions are contained in one book*' they reckon. I think that's true."

She placed her water bottle on top of the brochures then entered the spare room. A brief scan of the bookshelves revealed the object of her search—a small, well-thumbed paperback with a decorative purple jacket. She took it in hand and returned to the living area.

"Kiddo, this little story is the one," she said, taking up the customary horizontal couch position. "It's my absolute favourite. It helped me cope in the time before you came along. And I think it should be the very first book we read together."

*

From: "Tin Lid" <womb@almighty.com>
To: "Adam O'Doherty" <edam_odoh@fathertobe.com>
Subject: Story

Mum read me a story today. *The Alchemist*. It's about some shepherd boy called Santiago who leaves his sheep and goes in search of worldly treasure. Mum said it's about following your dream. She cried throughout most of it—I didn't think it was that bad.

Have you read it, too?

*

Lying in bed, pillow propped behind his back, sleeping wife nestled into his chest, the purple-jacketed novel in his right hand, Adam O'Doherty could easily recall his three previous readings of *The Alchemist*.

On each occasion he read it aloud, cover to cover. Maddy was his audience; a sometimes philosophical, sometimes inconsolable, and in History's third aftermath, seemingly irreparable Maddy. Throughout the initial chapters, every sentence delivered was a stone pitched at the blackened sky. By story's end, they were loose change tossed into a wishing well. Then, slowly, inexorably, over a period of time determined by a denied mother's unknowable criteria—days, weeks, on the third strike an even four months—a line from the opening page would take root once more:

'It's the possibility of having a dream come true that makes life interesting.'

Adam placed the novel on his bedside table and enveloped his wife with a double arm wrap. The dream had passed over possible; it was destined. Life had moved beyond interesting; it was joyous.

And Maddy was now the one reading aloud.

8

"'Daddy O'Doherty'...Edam, that definitely has a ring to it."

Kelly punched the ball down the middle of the service court causing Adam to stretch. The return limped over the net, inviting attack. Kelly walked forward two paces and drove the ball into the backhand corner. Again Adam stretched, again the ball flopped back into play. The sequence was repeated four more times—Kelly, stationary and zinging the ball side to side; Adam scrambling back and forth, each parry more feeble than the last—until the aggressor, perhaps mercifully, crushed the ball down the forehand line for a winner.

"You keep running me around like that," replied Adam, half-coughing and patting his sternum, "and I'll never get to be a Daddy."

Kelly defibrillated his chest with a pair of tennis balls and moved into position for his next serve. "Have you lined up the babysitters?" he asked.

"Babysitters!"

"You're gunna need time to write those bestsellers of yours, Edam. And Maddy'll want to go back to work after a while."

"She doesn't want to go back to work."

"Hey?"

"Maddy doesn't want to go back to Centrelink. She wants to stay at home."

"All the time?"

"All the time."

Kelly mulled the statement over while adjusting the strings of his racquet. "Good for her," he said finally, before thundering down another unplayable.

"Are you putting your hand up for child-minding duties?" asked Adam.

Kelly shrugged. "Yeah. I am. I mean, I know Aunty Mum and Uncle Dad'll be all over it like a rash. They'll probably have the little bludger more often than you guys. But when they're not around…and with Maddy's folks in Canada…"

"What makes you think a boofhead like you could take care of an infant?"

Kelly jutted his chin. "Everyone says I have a 'way' with children at the clinic. And before you open your gob, I know fifteen minute adjustments aren't the real deal. But I'm not intending to be surrogate 'Father of the Year', am I? Just a friendly, neighbourly, temporary carer—that's my job description. And, in the end, it's an *infant*, Ed! They don't talk back. They can't run away. Nicking the car or bringing home jailbait squeezes doesn't enter the equation. All they do is eat, drink, pee, crap, cry and sleep. Just like my rellies at Christmas."

Adam extracted a ball lodged in the back netting and approached the service line. "Okay. How about we up the ante, Unkey Kel. Here's the deal: if I win the next set, you play parent for the next three weeks."

"How's that going to work? You gunna hire a kid for me off the internet?"

"Christ, no! Those Romanian orphans have been through enough already! No, I was thinking more along the lines of self-raising parenthood. You could be Daddy to the old three kilo bag of flour."

Kelly bounced from foot to foot. "Like they done on 'Frasier'?"

"In the prisons, too, if I'm not mistaken."

"So, I don't have to worry about the eating, drinking, peeing, etcetera. I just have to keep the little fella in sight and intact."

"Yes. Much like *you* at Christmas."

Kelly nodded. "Well, it's a tempting offer," he said, turning his Nike cap backwards, "but unfortunately Lleyton's back in da house. COME ON!!!"

Adam tossed the ball and pounded out his best serve of the evening—a skidder at the body that the receiver could only fend off into the side netting.

"Papa Lleyton!" he shouted. "That definitely has a ring to it!"

*

From: "Tin Lid" <womb@almighty.com>
To: "Adam O'Doherty" <edam_odoh@fathertobe.com>
Subject: New Dad

After getting skanked, your friend Kelly is making good on his promise, hey? His voice is bright and chipper and full of 'coo-coo' noises. Is raising a bag of flour his dream?

*

From: "Adam O'Doherty" <edam_odoh@fathertobe.com>
To: "Tin Lid" <womb@almighty.com>
Subject: Re: New Dad

No, his dream is still to make the *Guinness Book of Records* for flipping the most beer coasters.

He has made a very positive start to parenthood, however. Attentive, loving. When the red Monaro pulled into the driveway he had Dougie Defiance (that's the little snapper's name) sitting beside him in the front seat, propped up on a couple of phone books, seat belt securely fastened. And when he departed, he only drove a few yards before realizing he'd left the lad on the roof.

Dougie Defiance.

Quite a striking looking child. Seventies'-style afro wig. Permanent smile. One eye double the size of the other (I think the texta might've slipped). With that box-shaped body and a head full of soft, squishy contents, there's no question he takes after his father. Little wonder he's so proud.

*

Maddy placed the phone on the coffee table, stood up on the couch and cheered.

"Guess what, Kiddo!" she said, punting a cushion at the latest character reincarnation on 'Days Of Our Lives', "That was Dawn on the phone and she says it's okay for your mother to start moving around a bit more! How about that? Fantastic, hey! What's that? You're worried I might do too much? Perish the thought! I'm not going to go out and run a marathon now that we're free. Nuh-uh. The most we'll be doing is the odd walk. Give you a chance to experience a world other than 150 James Street."

She stepped down from the couch and noted the date on the 'Canadian Rockies' calendar by the fridge.

"We're going to go shopping tomorrow, Kiddo. And I think we might invite a special guest along."

Maddy returned to the coffee table, grasped the phone and punched in the number for Carsmair State High School.

*

Adam paused in front of a dilapidated 1920s Queenslander with two restored Valiants in the front yard. Maddy marched several paces on, realised she was alone and backtracked.

"What's up, guy? Is the pace too hot for you? I'm the one who's supposed to be out of shape you know."

Adam removed his Ray-Bans. "Let me get this straight: we're going to the 'Pregnancy, Birth and Baby Expo' at the Convention Centre."

"That's what I said, yes."

"Tomorrow."

"Yes."

"And...you asked Jay-Jay to come along."

"Yes, I did."

Adam snorted and ran a hand through his sweat-sprinkled hair. "What did she say?"

"She said she'd come. We're meeting her there around eleven."

"Was she surprised to get an invite?"

"Surprised? Hmm...when I told her about it there was a long pause then an awful clatter. I think she might've dropped the phone."

"Is that right?"

"More likely it was just an accident though. Clumsiness goes with the territory of being pregnant."

"Yeah, well she has been tripping over tongue lately."

Maddy stretched her calves. "She was quite enthusiastic by the end. She said it's never too early to start preparing for a baby's arrival."

"Indeed."

The couple resumed walking. 'Orb Hair', 'Hair Today' and 'Seattle Hair' drifted by on the journey down Merthyr Road. With its inordinate proportion of Mediterranean mullets and Gay-Boy tints, Adam imagined New Farm offered more hairdressing salons per head of population than any other suburb in Brisbane, possibly Australia. And right now, trailing his born-again, high-stepping wife, he felt in a position to add one more to that number. True, he barely knew the business end of a blowdryer. But the gossip currently swirling in and around his life could've paid the rent for a year.

Or perhaps two.

"Shelley rang today. Wanted to know who our doctor was."

It was Maddy's turn to stop. "What did you say to that?"

"I told her straight up—I said we don't have one. I said we were going with a midwife."

"What did *she* say to that?"

"Not much. Nothing negative. I got the impression she wasn't too thrilled."

"That's hardly news is it?" Maddy pulled her shoulders back and strode onward. Adam enlisted a quick jog to catch up. "As far as Michelle's concerned, the medical expertise of the mainstream—the same expertise she will soon begin to acquire—is the only option for Mums-to-be. It has hundreds of years and billions of dollars behind it. It brings countless healthy little babies into the world and rescues countless more from tragedy. It performs miracles on a daily basis. It represents the only true peace of mind. It couldn't possibly screw up."

Adam intercepted his wife's hand. A gentle but insistent squeeze prompted Maddy to halt.

"Shell's just looking out for you," he said. "She doesn't want to cause trouble."

"I know."

"I mean, if she knew-"

"I *know* she *doesn't know*, Adam. I know."

Adam kissed the wedding band that had bound them for better or for worse nine years ago. Engraved onto its golden veneer was a Native American depiction of an eagle—symbol of power and connection to the Great Spirit.

"Maybe it's time she *did* know."

Maddy laughed and scanned her husband from head to toe. "You're a worry gorgeous, handsome man. All this 'Wanting to Tell' business, the pregnancy and now our History. Not usually the stuff of regular blokes, is it?"

"Come on, Mad. You know as well as I do that this would bring things full circle. It would bring closure."

"It would, Oprah, yes."

"And I've never claimed to be a regular bloke."

Maddy moved in close, stood on both of Adam's Converse-sneakered feet, and pinched his cheeks.

"Thank God for that."

As she headed for the James Street crosswalk, she added:

"I just have to find the right moment."

It occurred to Adam he'd heard that somewhere before.

*

From: "Tin Lid" <womb@almighty.com>
To: "Adam O'Doherty" <edam_odoh@fathertobe.com>
Subject: Just The Thing

Phew! What a day! A thousand 'Expo' people (do you call them 'Exposers'?) offering their help, telling you and Mum about how they've got 'just the thing' for me. Just the thing to eat. Just the thing to wear. Just the thing to get me laughing. Just the thing to stop me crying. Just the thing to have me learning my ABCs and just the thing to have me accepting the toilet as my pal. All the things to ensure I fulfill my 'most valuable potential' or some crap like that. And all for a very special price because Mum's pregnant and Dad looks like a 'discerning consumer' and the warehouse is overstocked and the next shipment from Italy doesn't arrive for two months.

Right now, a lie down is just the thing for me.

Hey, did your friend give up her secret? I sensed some whispers and murmurs about it. I also heard a booming voice call her name followed by cheers and whistles and pee-in-the-pants laughter.

*

"I need to have a word with you."

Adam immediately recognised the signs—knotted brow, pinched mouth, monotone speech, hands cuffed behind the back.

The 'Trance'.

Jenna Grimson descended into The Trance for especially sticky challenges. Adam had witnessed the spectacle twice before; once when she'd been required to teach a Metalwork unit; the second time when railroaded into 'Hey Big Spender' at a Vietnamese karaoke bar. And now here it was, once more to the fore, in front of the Nursing Mothers' Association booth at the 'Pregnancy, Birth and Baby Expo'.

"There's a little...situation that you should be aware of."

Adam glanced at Boyd. Desultory Dad had his own trance going, eyes glued to a nearby poster. It displayed a pair of exposed, faceless breasts with the caption: *'Give your baby the best take-away. Two convenient locations.'* Adam elbowed him in the ribs.

"This is coming out of left field, Mad."

*

Maddy swiveled away from a 'Jolly Jumper: Dos and Don'ts video and warily attended to her Expo sidekick.

'Left field'—not a happy place of origin. Not at this time, not in these circumstances. Her own left field had invariably offered cloistered pain and irresistible evacuation and useless pleas and the world falling apart.

Was Jenna in trouble? Had trouble already speared into tragedy? Maddy recalled she'd dropped the phone when asked to come along today; an occurrence, at the time, attributable to bog-standard clumsiness. Was there a far graver cause? Jen certainly wasn't herself right now. You only had to look at the goldfish face she was presently wearing to know that was true.

The potential sadness of the prevailing context suddenly became apparent to Maddy: Jay, though betrayed by Fate, stays loyal to a friend's invitation. Why? Because she can't come up with any sort of lie? Because loyalty, unlike pregnancy, has the capacity to remain solid and steadfast and reliable if one so desires? Maybe she's swallowed the insulting, throwaway rhetoric that inevitably comes your way post-loss:

Be strong!

Move on!

Put it behind you!

Sure, it's not an easy invitation Jenna's honouring. A visit to the 'Pregnancy, Birth and Baby Expo' could easily be construed as an act of masochism. But what better place to start afresh, hey? What better opportunity to nip that pesky grieving process in the bud?

Happens to lots of women!

Climb back on the horse!

No time like the present!

GO ON, GET ON WITH YOUR LI---

Maddy scrunched her eyes, shooed the sniping thoughts

from her mind. Rationality gained a moment's freedom. She recognised this knee-jerk panic for what it was: History's doing, nothing more. Left field ought not be feared. It harboured the unexpected; not necessarily doom. It could just as easily engineer diversion or distraction. Perhaps even joy.

Jenna Grimson was 'with child' and anything was possible.

As the PA crackled to life overhead, Maddy opened her eyes and smiled, toying with the idea that her treasured, goldfish-faced friend had twins on board.

*

"THE WINNER...OF THE DOOR PRIZE...IN OUR 'BOUNCING BABY BASKET' DRAW IS...JENNA GRIMSON!!!

The Trance twitched, contorted, broke down into dazed despair.

"JENNA GRIMSON—OUR LUCKY WINNER!"

Lucky Winner looked at Maddy, at the stage, at Boyd---

"JENNA?"

---at the stage, at Adam, at the stage---

"C-57?"

---at the ticket in her purse, at the stage, back at Maddy. A wan smile accompanied a small jiggle of the cursed stub.

"I did say left field, didn't I?"

The chosen recipient of a hamper advertising the promise of 'Everything a new mother could want!' shuffled off toward her prize.

"I wonder if there's a fake belly in there?" mused Adam, desperately clinging to a straight face.

"Or a 'Come clean' voucher," muttered Boyd.

*

Adam's stomach backflipped as his e-mail inbox appeared on the computer screen.

Checking incoming messages was a twice-daily event now. The ongoing prospect of connecting with his child, of rising above the mundane and engaging with a miracle, was a privilege beyond the lip service of once a week, or even once a day. It asked for a commitment worthy of its own munificent constancy.

Constancy.

That's what made this so special.

Adam had experienced miracles before. The times when Maddy reached into his soul with a touch or a look or a laugh. When words he'd assembled took flight and shone like the constellations. When a small stick had shown the O'Dohertys to be pregnant for the fourth and most unlikely time. These were moments of transcendence, and Adam felt blessed to have tasted their wonder. Yet they were sporadic gifts, unfettered by rites or routine, to be regarded with the same reverence as a last mortal meal.

Little B's correspondence wasn't like that. It was surety, certainty. Constancy. The ultimate indicator of destiny's drive, of the masterplan's progression.

And clicking on the unopened e-mail from Tristan titled *'Good News About Your Novel'*, Adam believed the masterplan *was* progressing, no question about it.

*

From: "Adam O'Doherty" <edam_odoh@fathertobe.com>
To: "Tin Lid" <womb@almighty.com>
Subject: Closer

My agent Tristan e-mailed to tell me I got two rejections for *The Ordinary Man's Enemy*—one from Eaton & Barry, the other from Costigan Press. He isn't fazed. According to him 'It's all good'. E&B, he claims, are too big to appreciate a work like this, whilst Costigan Press are too selective for their own good. He wasn't surprised by this outcome. He can't wait to see them kick themselves when the novel goes bestseller with somebody else, in all likelihood Hutton House or Kendrick & Sons.

How do *I* regard this news?

I am two rejections closer to my triumph.

9

Maddy emptied a bucket of grass clippings into the compost bin and gave voice to the questions shunting her regular trains of thought:

"Would you like to have a doctor, Kiddo? Hey? Would you like a doctor to watch over you and keep you from harm?"

She patted her abdomen.

"Your Aunty Michelle would. Probably the rest of Daddy's family, too. I know where they're coming from, but I won't let doctors be responsible for you. I won't have them telling me everything's fine and everything's gone with the exact same face. Assuring me there are plenty of women worse off than yours truly. Reminding me they never made any promises or guarantees. I won't have them pretending they care. I won't. Never again."

She prodded the compost with a pitchfork then sat down heavily in a nearby garden chair.

"The O'Dohertys need to understand where *I'm* coming from."

Maddy extracted the phone from her hip pocket. She punched out six numbers, paused, stabbed the 'Off' button. After a few deep breaths, she repeated the process, this time managing to complete the required eight number sequence. The disconnection severed the second set of beeps. Maddy tapped the appliance against the forehead.

"Sorry."

A shrill scream of frustration preceded a slow, contemplative shuffle toward the rear stairs of the house.

*

From: "Adam O'Doherty" <edam_odoh@fathertobe.com>
To: "Tin Lid" <womb@almighty.com>
Subject: Saved by the...

At the family dinner this evening, it took two hours and two serves of Grandad's infamous beef and black bean goulash for *the* question to be tabled.

Such a long wait had seemed unlikely at the commencement of proceedings. Chit-chat from the outset had revolved around one topic and one topic alone...

*

"I can't imagine a better job than obstetrician," raved Michelle, responding to group misgivings about blood and forceps and abusive women in the clutches of agony. "Every day the privilege of greeting new life at the world's front door."

*

From: "Adam O'Doherty" <edam_odoh@fathertobe.com>
To: "Tin Lid" <womb@almighty.com>
Subject: Saved by the...

...Here we go, I thought. Family Dinner is set to become Family Feud.

A tick of the clock ensued. Then another. Then several more. At the bottom of the hour, suggestions for a male equivalent of labour—"Pushing a rubber chicken through the front!"... "Passing a watermelon out the back!"...—circumnavigated the table.

The room was like an over-inflated balloon. I sussed the other main players; they were feeling the pressure, too. Shell couldn't go ten seconds without glancing in our direction. Maddy refused to lift her eyes from the zebra motif tablecloth. Something had to give. Some*one* had to give.

I didn't think it would be Chris...

*

"Too bad you weren't finished your course already, Michelle.

You could've been Maddy's doctor. Who *is* your doctor, guys?"

*

From: "Adam O'Doherty" <edam_odoh@fathertobe.com>
To: "Tin Lid" <womb@almighty.com>
Subject: Saved by the...

...This wasn't the *right moment*. Deflection was essential. Doctor Zhivago? Doctor Seuss? Doctor Kevorkian? I cleared my throat, opened my mouth to speak then felt your mum's hand on my right arm...

*

Maddy cocked her head several degrees but maintained her focus on the tablecloth.

"No doctors. Our midwife will take care of our child."

Silence descended over the party. Reg and Eileen abandoned their jolly family host faces for their rarely seen serious-parent dials. Chris wiped his mouth with the napkin from his lap. Michelle joined her hands and brought them up under her chin. Woody, constantly moving during his half hour scab-grab of dinner scraps, dropped to the floor, head on his front paws.

*

From: "Adam O'Doherty" <edam_odoh@fathertobe.com>
To: "Tin Lid" <womb@almighty.com>
Subject: Saved by the...

...I knew they couldn't leave it at that. They wanted elaboration. And there was no shortage of things that ought to be said: *This was not a decision we took lightly. There are reasons for it. Compelling and valid reasons. Reasons pertaining to an unspeakable History. And, anyway, what's the big deal about giving the doctor a miss? Hadn't women been giving birth for thousands of years before the all-knowing, all-seeing, all-powerful obstetrician came on the scene?*

I said none of it. Muteness took over with another touch to my arm, but this time it wasn't Maddy.

It was a smiley, grubby, afro-sporting, wonky-eyed 'child', now patched up with Elastoplast, speechless as the man whose hide he was about to save...

*

"Good on you, Maddy. Sandy and I never needed a doctor for young Dougie here. A checkout chick, yes, but no doctor."

*

From: "Adam O'Doherty" <edam_odoh@fathertobe.com>
To: "Tin Lid" <womb@almighty.com>
Subject: Saved by the...

I could've kissed Kelly. Invited for comic relief, he'd taken his cue with great aplomb. And it soon became apparent he'd engineered something much more substantial than mere diversion.

Dougie Defiance now held court.

Every aspect of the little urchin's short life came under scrutiny. How old was he? Had he spoken any words yet? Did he have a thing going with Isabella Icing Sugar? Was he a big fan of Bread? By the time photo opportunities were exhausted and the recount of his latest misadventure—a near fatal mishap with the Clark pool's filter—was complete, the clock indicated it was going home time and the No Doctor controversy had gone the way of Reg's leftover goulash.

After this difficult incident, B, perhaps Mum will now allow me to give Michelle a call?

*

Maddy stood in front of the recliner, obstructing view of Channel Ten's broadcast of *Groundhog Day*. A prostrate Adam pulled the lever at the side of the chair and sat up straight.

"Okay, Sir Fix-A-Lot. For the last time…what am I?"

"You are my loving wife."

"And what am I not?"

"You are not a damsel in distress."

"What are you?"

"I am your loving husband."

"And what are you not?"

"I am not a knight in shining armour."

"Can you slay every dragon I come across?"

"No, I can't."

"Should you *try* to slay every dragon I come across?"

"No, I shouldn't."

"What must you do instead?"

"I must be an atypical guy who has enough confidence and trust in his wife's abilities to snuff the dragon on her own."

Maddy produced a small curtsy. "Thank you, good sir."

As she returned to the kitchen table and her draft design of the nursery, she added: "I rang Shell and invited her over for brunch on Thursday. In the meantime, if you must be chivalrous, help Jenna out at school tomorrow. She rang before. Wanted some writing advice."

*

Jenna retrieved a crumpled piece of A4 from her briefcase and smoothed it out on her thigh.

"I hate having to do this by correspondence, Ad. I've written a dozen opening lines and all of them are absolute crap."

"They can't be that bad."

"'*Guess which one of us isn't getting fatter!*'"

"Ah."

"'*Using a Paddle-Pop stick for my pregnancy test was a mistake.*'"

"Okay, they can't *all* be that bad."

"'*A funny thing happened on the way to having a baby... I shouldn't have had sex with The Phantom... When I said I was "with child" I was actually talking about being married to Boyd...*'"

"Apart from the last one, I stand corrected."

She gave Adam a push to the shoulder. "You're the writer. Help me out here."

"Mmm...how about '*The following is a story of immaculate misconception...*'"

"I'll get a pencil."

Adam grabbed her hand and gave it a pat. "Jen, there is nothing—I repeat *nothing*—for you to be anxious about. Maddy will not only understand, she will be *grateful*. Circumstances meant things had to be kept under wraps, and when I stuffed up you stepped in like a true friend would. You saved Maddy's feelings and my arse. Now that those circumstances are finished, everyone, including you, ought to be happy and safe and comfortable. Here, give me that paper." He scribbled down his recommended introduction in bold block letters. "There's your opener."

Jay-Jay read it, turned the paper over, turned it back again. "*'I'M NOT PREGNANT!'*"

"Yep."

"That's it?"

"Yep."

"I'm not pregnant."

"Just say it. Straight up."

Jenna sighed then folded the paper into quarters. "Bloody Expo bloody door prize."

*

From: "Adam O'Doherty" <edam_odoh@fathertobe.com>
To: "Tin Lid" <womb@almighty.com>
Subject: The Question of Dregs

School today produced a curly student question:

"Hey sir! In a few years time, will you be teaching your *own* kid?"

The inquirer was a year nine lad, Toby O'Reagan. Better known to all at Carsmair High as 'Dregs'. Up till then, I'd assumed, quite naively, that the student body knew nothing about my imminent Dadhood. Up till then, I'd also assumed, also quite naively, that Dregs' math was improving.

"I'm not sure?" I replied, taking time-out from my poor impression of a playground monitor. "What do you think, pal?"

Dregs ran a hand over his freshly shaved skull then produced some sort of rap move that looked like 'Hang loose!' but probably meant 'You're a dopey bugger!'

"I think it's cert, man! And I think you can't wait!"

"You reckon I'll be a teacher that long?"

"I reckon you'll be a teacher for another two decades! Maybe even another twenty years!"

I'm always amused when students assume I'm a career chalkie. Relieved, too, because it means they haven't yet exposed me as a charlatan.

Another person who won't be teaching his own kid is Kelly. We're heading over there for a celebration drinks tonight. Because he's been such a fine father, I've given Kel early parole on his three weeks. He's celebrating by baking a cake in Dougie's honour. No prizes for guessing the main ingredient.

*

Cat Stevens' 'Father And Son' meandered out of the stereo's surround-sound speakers and filled the available spaces of Kelly and Sandy Clark's rumpus room. The host sang along, drawling the drawls and wailing the wails, occasionally sipping from the can of Bundy and Coke in his hand. Sandy waited for the second verse before taking up a platter of nibblies and approaching Adam.

"Care for some?"

"No thanks."

"They're for throwing."

Adam selected a smoked oyster on a water cracker and two pieces of celery dipped in hommus.

"You reckon he's ready now to be a real Dad?" he inquired.

"Not quite yet."

"He did a good job with Dougie, Sand. Okay, the little guy took a few spills, but that's kids for you. Look at him over there!" Kel's gentle air guitar riffing had given way to a cigarette lighter sway. "That's some parental emotion right there!"

"He should be emotional. It's the fifth kid he's lost in three weeks."

"Hey?"

Sandy placed the platter down on the coffee table and picked up a muffin from the adjoining tray. "These are Dougie

Number One," she said. "Sadly, on the third of March, he was left out on the deck railing overnight." She took a small bite then pointed to a plate of chocolate chip cookies on the breakfast bar. "Those are Dougie Two. Regrettably, he slipped from Dad's grasp during a game of 'Upsy-Daisy' on the seventh." She handed Adam the remaining muffin portion. "The other two Dougies didn't make the menu. Three was attacked by crows at the park and Four remains missing in action, somewhere between here and the Mitchelton Mitre 10."

"You're kidding, aren't you?"

Sandy applauded her husband's attempt at a falsetto finish and folded her arms. "It's lucky you gave him a few days grace. We might've ended up with the baker's half dozen."

"But I saw the state Dougie was in tonight. Dirty. Taped up. Bashed around. Are you telling me that…"

Sandy nodded. "His attention to detail was terrific. Each replacement had to be exactly the same as his fallen predecessor. Same dirt. Same tape. Same amount of bashing around. It wasn't easy, I can tell you. He just about had to back the car over Dougie Five to get him looking wrecked enough."

"That sneaky bastard!"

"The time he put into cloning, if he'd spent that time actually minimising the risk to the little nipper and keeping him out of situations where he could get trashed…well, the original Dougie might've gone the distance."

The oven timer rang out across the kitchen, indicating the cake was done. Kel turned the stereo down, opened his hands in a 'Dearly Beloved' gesture of piety, and sauntered off to eat the first slice of his last child.

"Why didn't he tell me?" asked Adam. "I mean, it's not like there were sheep stations riding on this. It's not like it was a *real* kid."

Sandy leaned closer and softened her voice. "It probably sounds silly, but he couldn't work up the gumption,

Adam. Kelly's good at a lot of things—you know that. His chiropractic, his study, golf, tennis, telling jokes, talking to people, partying…there isn't much he can't do, and he's proud of that fact. But this was beyond him. Something you don't need a licence or qualifications for, something seemingly anyone could do, something a lot of young kids could probably do standing on their heads…it was too much for him. That is, with the exception of the crows—that was just the worst kind of luck. The rest of the time it was beyond him. And he tried. He really did. He just couldn't get it done." Sandy looped an arm through Adam's. "He didn't tell you or anyone else because he didn't want to be seen as a failure. Does that sound silly?"

Adam observed Maddy, seated at the dining table, gratefully accepting a generous slice of Death By Chocolate from Kel. For someone with a 'Dragon Date' the next morning, she was more than prepared to take her chances with a lethal cake tonight.

"It doesn't sound silly at all," he replied.

10

From: "Tin Lid" <womb@almighty.com>
To: "Adam O'Doherty" <edam_odoh@fathertobe.com>
Subject:

Mum is crying. Hard. She's trying to speak, but she can't put any words together. Her breaths are shallow, fast. Each one is like a squeeze on my soul.

Jeez, why did I have to wake up now?

Aunty Shelley is there. She's on the phone. Her voice is strong and clear. And dark. Dark as the thoughts crowding around me. She repeats the words 'five minutes', then hangs up. She moves close.

"It's not always bad," she says. "This sort of thing can happen for no reason."

Mum falls against her.

"I understand, Mad," she says. I don't think she does.

The dragon isn't slain yet, is it?

*

From: "Tin Lid" <womb@almighty.com>
To: "Adam O'Doherty" <edam_odoh@fathertobe.com>
Subject:

What's going on now? I'm confused. And scared.

This is not our home. The sounds are weird. Buzzes, beeps, bells. A voice commands from above. Aunty Shelley is gone, but others speak to each other, without warmth or laughter or comfort. They seem to speak through closed windows. I don't recognize these people. I want to hide from them.

But they're close now. Real close. Too close. Mum is still crying, but she's also angry.

"I will decide," she says. "Not you!"

A man called 'Registrar' states very firmly that 'This cannot continue,' and argues she is 'not acting in the best interest of all'.

"It is in my best interest that you leave me alone!" she says.

The man declares that 'someone else can try to reason with her' and no more is said.

Where are you in all this, Dad? Are you there? Please reply. Please help me understand what is going on. Please tell me things will get better.

*

From: "Tin Lid" <womb@almighty.com>
To: "Adam O'Doherty" <edam_odoh@fathertobe.com>
Subject:

I asked the Supremo if our lines of communication had been closed, if my messages were no longer permitted to get through to you:

Correspondence may be disallowed when it conflicts with an opportunity to learn.

Is there a conflict?

No.

Okay, so my words are with you, but you do not want to respond to them. Why? Why now?

Mum has stopped crying, but sadness is still tearing at her heart. A woman is trying to talk to her now. A kind woman. She 'wants to apologise for her colleague yesterday' and indicates she is there to listen and help.

"The person I trust to listen and help—to care—will be along shortly," replies Mum. "Same as yesterday. Same as tomorrow, the day after and the day after that."

The kind woman says her name is 'Sam' and promises to return later, just to 'touch base'.

I really need you, Dad. Have I done something wrong? Am I no longer wanted? If so, let's call this day 'Thursday' and start over.

I'm very tired. I don't want to sleep any more, but I have no choice.

Immovable

11

It was just after eight in the evening when Adam O'Doherty opened the front door of 150 James Street. Sixty-plus hours worth of baked air rushed to find space beyond the walls of the house, carrying with it the leftover captive whiffs of disturbance and desperation. He entered, tossed his school briefcase onto the recliner and went to the bathroom. He splashed water on his face. Ignoring the haggard image in the mirror, he patted dry with his wife's towel and proceeded to check the phone messages. There were five. They could easily have been merged into one:

"It's me. Just ringing to see if you'd like to have dinner over here...that is if you want to...understand totally if you'd rather not...call if there's anything else we can do... bye for now."

Adam left the answering machine on and cooked one of the half-dozen Beef Stroganoff dinners in the freezer. Whilst eating in silence, CNN's parade of war experts informed him, in a dozen different ways, that the enemy's ownership of weapons of mass destruction was undeniable and that any word to the contrary was attributable to an unhinged mind.

At 10:16, he ditched the news, entered the spare room and approached the computer. After fifteen minutes and one hundred paces holding the lion-serpent bottle opener, he sat down to log on.

*

From: "Adam O'Doherty" <edam_odoh@fathertobe.com>
To: "Tin Lid" <womb@almighty.com>
Subject:

Are you awake?

Please say you have woken up.

Please please please say you are there.

*

From: "Tin Lid" <womb@almighty.com>
To: "Adam O'Doherty" <edam_odoh@fathertobe.com>
Subject:

Yes, I'm here.

*

From: "Adam O'Doherty" <edam_odoh@fathertobe.com>
To: "Tin Lid" <womb@almighty.com>
Subject:

Two words have allowed me to breathe again.

I am writing this from our home, B. You are not at home. You are in ward 4C of the Galbraith Private Hospital, twenty minutes drive from where I sit. You have been there since half past one on Thursday. I arrived about half an hour after your mother's admission and remained there until two hours ago. For me—the last two and a half days have been a fingertip hold on the precipice of Purgatory. For you—reading your e-mails, I can only imagine it was a plunge into Hell itself.

I am so, so sorry. For not replying. For not answering your pleas. For not assuaging your fear. You asked if you had done something wrong? The only person guilty of wrongdoing in all of this is yours truly.

*

Adam withdrew his fingers from the keyboard and studied the unfinished sentence on screen. He had no excuses. There were PCs at the hospital; technology that could have been accessed with a request or an appeal or a beg. He could've continued 'The Umbilical Word' dialogue if he'd wanted to.

He'd justified not wanting to.

What if there was no message from B? Meeting Maddy's eye would be nigh impossible. As it was, he had hardly spoken to her (What words could possibly be said? *'It'll be alright'*? *'It may not happen this time'*? *'There are others worse off than us'*?) and holding her hand was all the usefulness he'd been able to muster from memory. In light of such token support, how could he then refuse to look at her? Abandon the courage required to glimpse the dagger lodged in her soul? What help could he possibly be if every meaningless object in the room became necessary distractions to his wife's tears? He had to be strong. For Maddy's sake, he would stay with her and ignore the Inbox.

It had been a lie. He'd been afraid. Weak. He'd chosen silence because he hadn't wanted his own pain—a pittance next to his child's, a speck of dust next to his wife's—to return.

*

From: "Adam O'Doherty" <edam_odoh@fathertobe.com>
To: "Tin Lid" <womb@almighty.com>
Subject:

...Please forgive me, B. I will not let you down again.

*

From: "Tin Lid" <womb@almighty.com>
To: "Adam O'Doherty" <edam_odoh@fathertobe.com>
Subject:

It's okay.

I think I let you down, too, Dad—I should've trusted you more. This was an opportunity to learn trust, you know?

I've learned a lesson.

I won't doubt you again, Dad.

*

Adam closed his mail, exited 'The Umbilical Word' file and wiped his eyes with the sleeve of his polo shirt.

Had he learned a lesson, too?

He knew this much—no one could be blamed for what was occurring. Maddy, in accordance with History's precedent, would continue to beat herself up over things that should or should not have been done. But she wasn't responsible. An event like this was beyond anyone's control. An event like this was *their* opportunity to learn trust.

Faith was the requirement. Faith in the masterplan, in Destiny.

Faith in their child.

Adam headed for bed, sleep now a necessary chore. Dawn Marks would be swinging by the hospital at seven thirty in the morning and he wanted to be there at least twenty minutes early. Maddy had gone to Galbraith because Dawn insisted she go, but since being admitted she had point blank refused to let any doctor touch her; their arguments for scans and tests and common sense bouncing off her like rubber bullets. And now, after three days, Adam sensed she was starting to feel vindicated. The bleeding, the 'spotting', the scourge, was not worsening—perhaps might've even thinned a little—and Dawn's examinations had not unearthed additional causes for alarm.

He wasn't about to second-guess Maddy's freeze out of the establishment but a thawing couldn't be entirely discounted. He recalled a doctor by the name of Samantha Pole dropping by twice yesterday, each time free of judgement and wearing kid gloves. Given the bedside manner of some of the practitioners in their experience (approaches that approximated a vulture standing over roadkill), they were welcome visitations. And the head nurse suggested they might continue for the duration of Maddy's stay. However long that duration might be.

"Let's make it one more day only, little B," murmured Adam, turning the bedside light out and rolling over into unoccupied bedspace that felt like barren earth. "Those tiny legs and arms you're now growing—twist 'em, turn 'em, lift 'em, shake 'em...show everyone you're strong. And then Mum can come home."

12

"Can I go home now?"

Dawn Marks instructed Maddy to pull her shirt down, sat back and placed her hands in her lap. Her eyes were more bulbous then ever, seemingly ready to leap from their sockets.

"On the whole, how are you feeling?"

"Bit funny."

"Pain?" asked the attentive, white-coated woman at the foot of the bed.

"No."

"Bad funny?" asked Adam.

"No. Not bad bad. Sort of squirmy." Maddy sat up a little straighter and cast a contemptuous eye at the breakfast tray. "Probably that atrocious excuse for an omelette they gave me for breakfast."

The midwife addressed the woman in the white coat. "Still stable you think, Doctor Pole?"

Doctor Samantha Pole—graduate of UQ and resident gynaecologist of Galbraith Private Hospital for three years—tugged at her earlobe and nodded once. "From what evidence we've got, yes."

"So how long *do* I have to stay in this quackhouse then?"

Adam noted the folded arm wrap Maddy had clamped across the small swell of her tummy. It was like an amulet, warding off evil hospital spirits and stethoscope-brandishing demons.

"A little while yet," replied the midwife. "I know you don't think so, but you need this place right now, Madeline.

It's a 'B and B'—'Bed and Bed'! Off your feet for everything bar powdering the nose. Those tiny things you thought risky but couldn't help doing when you were at home alone on the couch? They're irrelevant now. Someone else is doing them. The getting the glass of water and the extra blanket. And the lovely omelette!" She squeezed her patient's hand. "And besides, you wouldn't want to insult Doctor Pole's hospitality!"

"What do you mean?"

"Well, you wouldn't be here but for Doctor Pole. She's taken you on as a patient, even though I'm the one examining you."

"But for her, you would've been drop-kicked out of Galbraith on Friday," added Adam.

"Oh no! How awful!" Maddy stared her husband down, then made eye contact with the medico. "I guess I should thank you then." She extended a hand. The other arm remained steadfast against her abdomen. "Thank you, Doctor Pole."

The gynaecologist smiled and accepted, matching Maddy's firm business-like grip. "No problem. And you can call me Sam if it's more comfortable for you."

After arranging follow-up appointments, the carers departed. Adam sat down on the edge of the bed.

"Doctor Pole's being very good about this, isn't she?" he said. "It can't be good for her professional standing to be seen twiddling her thumbs whilst an outsider runs the show. I'm pretty sure the Registrar would consider her borderline negligent."

Maddy pressed the TV remote. "That arrogant bastard considers me over-the-borderline psycho."

*

"So what's going to happen at school tomorrow?"

Adam closed the tabloid magazine he'd bought (*Australia's 25 Most Inane People*) and looked at his watch. Visiting hours were almost over. He brought his chair bedside, took up Maddy's hand and stroked her fingers.

"I think it'll be ugly," he confided. "I told The Sarge what was going on when I left on Thursday. He would've briefed the Science staffroom on Private O'Doherty's reasons for going AWOL and no doubt it's spread from there. I hope so anyway. Save re-living every little detail." He began massaging her palm. "Mad, people are probably going to ask about…visiting. What's your feeling…"

The pampered hand clenched.

"Visitors? Yes. I think visitors should come."

"Babe, you're crushing my fingers."

"They should see that there is no reason for concern. There isn't any reason for concern, is there?"

"Well…not much. Not as it relates to our child's situation anyway."

"They should see that everything is under control. Yes?"

"Babe, the fingers."

"Visitors must come. Must…come."

Adam was taken aback. Not by Maddy's death grip, but by her tone. The anger and sadness of the first few days had been replaced by flint-hard determination. The warrior mentality of his wife was hardly a novelty—six years of battling History had seen it called upon numerous times—but he couldn't recall ever observing this level of instant resolve. Her brown eyes were like primed fists. Her elf ears were sunburn red. The contracted muscles of her jaw had become the standout feature of a once open and inviting face.

Magic Maddy appeared...immovable.

He felt sorry for the prospective visitors. Tradition suggested they should be sources of joy or, at the very least, temporary escape. Tonics for the mind and spirit. The Maddy cum Terminator accepting their cards and flowers would regard them as a necessary endurance, much like a learner driver test or a prostate exam. It was a tough ask. Given these prevailing conditions, Adam doubted whether anyone would relish dropping by 4C.

After all, who would want to be tagged as the medicine rather than the honey?

*

"I don't care if she's grumpy, Ad. I have to visit her. It's my penance."

Adam paused in his 'Grateful Guest' sink duty, holding a handful of sudsy cutlery, waiting for a punchline. There wasn't one. He looked toward hubby. Boyd pressed the lid down on some Tupperware, allowing the patented freshness burp to provide his response.

"I think I might've jinxed her, Ad," continued Jenna. "You know, with that note."

"The note."

"Yes. Starting it with 'I'M NOT PREGNANT!'…that might be the reason why Maddy's in hospital. Maybe it jinxed her or put a curse on her...or something…stop looking at me like that!"

"Voodoo influence aside, you never gave it to me, Sweetheart! She never read it!"

"I'm not sure it matters. The fact that it was written at all…you know? It puts negative energy out there, out into the world. It's like that Indian saying Dilip told me one time: 'The farmer that sows bad seeds gets…crap crops'…or something. The way he said it was much more profound."

Jenna slumped down into an armchair and slapped the open TV guide down onto her face.

"Pregnancy is one of God's great miracles," she said, her sad voice emanating from the cover mug of Eddie McGuire. "If you don't treat it with the respect it deserves, there's hell to pay."

Five minutes later, on the stroke of nine-thirty, Jenna Grimson meandered off to bed.

"She's not feeling the best lately," confided Boyd over one for the road. "She might even give school the swerve tomorrow."

Adam fervently hoped she might see fit to swerve Maddy as well.

*

From: "Tin Lid" <womb@almighty.com>
To: "Adam O'Doherty" <edam_odoh@fathertobe.com>
Subject: Understanding

I'm stressing about Mum. I sensed recently that she was changing and, at the time, I thought the change was for the better. But listening today, her voice is, like, totally foreign to my ears. Low. Measured. Hard. Like a heartbeat, but hollow.

I heard plenty of it when Mum had her first visitor today.

In the lead-up, Mum and Doctor Pole—'Sam'—were discussing an apparent epidemic of something known as 'Wardrobe Malfunction'.

Then *he* came by...

*

"Ms O'Doherty, it is in the best interest of all that you have a psych evaluation."

Maddy held a hand up toward Sam Pole, waylaying the gynaecologist's retort. She poured a glass of water and drank. She held the last mouthful for a few seconds—sloshing it around, cheeks distended—then gulped it down. The Registrar continued:

"Ms O'Doherty, it is my opinion that you are demonstrating signs of emotional instability and depression, perhaps even paranoia. I've set up a referral for you with a fine psychiatrist here at Galbraith, Doctor Thornquist. He will provide a clearer picture of your mental state. He might also be able to help you with some medication. That will certainly-"

"It's Doctor Mitchell, right?"

Despite his preparedness for battle, the Registrar flinched. A small tug on the tartan bow-tie and a jut of the chin restored his composure. "That's right, yes."

"Doctor Mitchell, you ever wanted something with all your soul?"

"It is not in your best interest---"

"You must have, surely."

"This has no relevance---"

"Maybe a Gold Coast penthouse? A Mercedes?"

"Ms O'Doherty-"

"Maybe a six under par round of golf at Royal Brisbane? Or a hole-in-one at Royal Brisbane? Or maybe both! Yes, a hole-in-one in your six under par round of golf at Royal Brisbane!"

The Registrar pivoted on his heel, stopped, turned back again. "It's Royal Queensland, for God's sake!" he blurted. "Royal *Queensland*!"

Maddy drank more water.

"Of course it is," she said. "Now, Doctor Mitchell, in the pursuit of these most worthy of ambitions, if you were to, say, throw your sticks around or swear at your ball, if you were driven to park one of Royal Brisbane's little motorised carts in the lake or in the clubhouse when it seemed you would come up short of your goal, then the last person you would want in your face would be me. Why? Ask me."

The Registrar cast a pleading glance in his colleague's direction. A smirking Sam Pole held up a glass of water.

"Go on. Ask me. Don't be-"

"Okay, why? Why would you be the last person I would want…in my face?"

Maddy adjusted the pillow behind her back. "Because I've never picked up a golf stick in my life."

The Registrar held his hands up. "Is there a point to this diatribe?"

"The point is, Bruce," interjected Sam, "She won't be seeing the psychiatrist. As Maddy's overseeing physician, I believe there is no need for anything beyond her current care."

A momentary pause was ended by a sharp huff of breath. Florsheim footsteps commenced, trailed off, gave way to the loud 'gatump!' of the door.

"He should pay a visit to Doctor Thornquist," said Maddy, nodding empathetically. "He might be able to help him with some medication."

Sam Pole laughed. "No chance with the wardrobe."

*

From: "Tin Lid" <womb@almighty.com>
To: "Adam O'Doherty" <edam_odoh@fathertobe.com>
Subject: Understanding

...Dad, I get the feeling Doctor Pole is more than just a cool person helping someone in need. I think she understands the change in Mum.

Have you noticed the change? Is it freaking you at all?

*

From: "Adam O'Doherty" <edam_odoh@fathertobe.com>
To: "Tin Lid" <womb@almighty.com>
Subject: Re: Understanding

Don't worry, B. The change is temporary and it is for the best. Mum is just being extra protective, making sure you are getting the highest quality care whilst dealing with some difficult circumstances.

*

I wish you could have spent some time with me this evening. Dinner was with the very understanding couple of Sandy and Kelly Clark this evening. Without asking me, they clued into the very thing we need right now—optimism. No talk of hospitals or hard times. Just of things getting better and a trouble-free run home.

And whispering...

"I've bought a book, Ed." Kelly retrieved a sky blue paperback from the lavatory and handed it to Adam.

"*The Secrets of the Baby Whisperer*. You bought this?"

"When you want us to mind your little tyke," he said, rubbing his hands together, "we'll be up to speed."

Adam observed Sandy taking the Glad Wrap off a plate of mini caramel tarts. "You're reading this, too?"

"No, I prefer 'Wheels' magazine."

"Don't listen to her, Ed," warned Kel. "She's dead keen to mind your bub as well."

Sandy planted a tart in her husband's mouth and resumed her seat. "If Michael Jackson's unavailable, we'll be only too willing to fill in."

Adam turned the book over, noting the promotional pitch: '…reassuring, down-to-earth and often flying in the face of conventional wisdom'. Summed up his hosts to a tee.

"So, they were all out of The Secrets of the Muffin Whisperer, then?" he asked.

"Totally. Here, look at the subtitle—*How to Calm, Connect and Communicate with Your Baby*. Communicate!" Kelly scoffed. "Dunno what advice she's gonna have for that!"

"Maybe you write them e-mails."

"Nah. Text 'em on the mobile. They're all being born with giant thumbs these days."

*

From: "Adam O'Doherty" <edam_odoh@fathertobe.com>
To: "Tin Lid" <womb@almighty.com>
Subject: Re: Understanding

…No swerving permitted here—Sandy and Kel are a *must* to visit Maddy. Just the sort of folk she needs to have around right now.

And speaking of the sort of folk Mum needs, I just got off the phone with her family in Canada. You'll love them—Mirna and Dom's smiling, furniture consignment store faces; Uncle Jake's yellow 'Cool Bus' ('School Bus' with the 'S' and the 'H' scraped off) containing his mini-golf business and backpack of worldly possessions; Aunty Tammy's tarot card readings and special effects make-up artistry; the nephews and nieces…They called to see how I was going and to inform me they were cooking dinner and having it flown over. I told them things were fine, okay, good as could be expected, and that my dinner debts already far exceeded my capacity to repay.

Knowing Tammy had rung the hospital every night since admission (usually around eight, just after my departure for home), I asked if she'd noticed the change in Mum, too…

*

"Can't say I have. Mad seems calm and, from what she says, everything's under control."

"What about her voice. Anything funny there?"

"Funny ha-ha?"

"Strange. Unusual."

"Oh, 'Satan is my master!' kind of thing, eh?"

"Pretty much."

"No, none of that. The Dark Lord is happy to stick with Nick Cave and me." Tamara paused. "Is she wiggin' out over there?"

"Hey?"

"Is she twisting her head around and barfing up pea soup at the hospital?"

"No, no. She's just very…focused."

"Focused?"

"It's no major drama. I'm just…you know, making sure she's okay with you guys, too. Covering both ends."

There was the sound of a drawer opening, then the 'phwit-phwit' of a deck of cards being shuffled.

"I've done some readings about Maddy, eh," Tamara said with gravity. "You needn't worry. Titania's cards keep coming up with 'Flowers' beside the first drawn which is, like, healing and happiness after a long period of sorrow."

"Ti-tania?"

"And the 'Sun' keeps falling beside the 'Road', which is a good sign for the rest of the pregnancy."

"Is it? That's great. Tam, look, I'd better get going. Gotta be up early. Final day of school before the Easter holidays. Dedicated professional that I am."

"Your cards were interesting, Adam."

"Mine?"

"Oh yeah. Big mix of stuff. 'Whip', 'Star', 'Book', 'Snake', 'Coffin', 'Clover'…ups, downs. A real rollercoaster. And right now, it's hard to tell how it will all finish up. Go figure, eh?"

"Tam, you'll be the first to know if I come flying off the loop-de-loop."

*

From: "Adam O'Doherty" <edam_odoh@fathertobe.com>
To: "Tin Lid" <womb@almighty.com>
Subject: Re: Understanding

...Aunty Tammy has predicted McDonald's will go belly-up by Christmas 2010 and swears blind the next Pope will be a Swede. So let's hope her observed change of fortune for Mum is an aberration.

I wasn't lying to Aunt Tammy—school *is* out for the Easter holidays tomorrow. Ten days of parole awaits. No more health inquiries and background probes and personal guarantees and first hand, second hand, third hand stories of pregnancy near misses with happy endings. And, yes, I'm talking about the students as well as my colleagues. What is it with these kids? Why are my family goings-on a topic of discussion in the playground? Don't they have hormones?

Everyone means well, B, but give me the writer's lot. If you disappear suddenly, nobody has to see. If you encounter hardship, nobody has to know. No serious faces leaning over your desk or waiting for you at the water cooler or bailing you up on the basketball court. No earnest voices asking if I'm okay and if I'm taking my mind off things and if I'm keeping cool in the crunch.

It's just you and your creation's assurances that things are never as bad as they seem.

13

Maddy's assessment of her voluntary shift to a spare bed in the Intensive Care Ward:

It was the second best thing that could have happened.

The staff at 4C had been most agreeable to washing their hands of 'The Scary O'Doherty Woman'. The Scary Woman herself couldn't have cared less and had jumped at the chance of a move. A second longer with the all too familiar fallout of those denied a child and the offensive ambivalence of those denying the possibility of any more was a second too long. And the further she distanced herself from *the* room—the one she'd had in '99, the one post-'procedure'—the better. That faulty buzzer, those faded floral curtains, the view of the Brisbane River that suggested the world could be a sunny and hospitable host when clearly it was nothing of the sort.

Yes, the shift was a positive. It may have paled in comparison with the best of all outcomes—a wave goodbye and a finger gesture to this godforsaken hospital—but it did mean dossing down in a History-free zone.

That was an intensive care of sorts.

*

"Adam's Aunty Dolores just got a tattoo of the family crest on her shoulder..."

"Our Rock 'N Roll dance teacher reckons we've lost weight..."

"Woody had a go at the postie again..."

Adam studied Maddy's demeanour with his parents. She

nodded and shook her head on cue. She delivered responses in less than ten words. Her eyeline barely shifted from the plastic patient's bracelet on her right wrist.

No worse.

No better either.

For all intents and purposes, his folks hadn't clued in to Maddy's altered persona, or if they had they weren't mentioning it. Indeed, they seemed unwilling to admit their very presence in a hospital. Reg's comment that 'Intensive Care rooms had more space than Neil Armstrong and more plugs than Elton John' was the extent of their acknowledgement. The foursome could just as easily have been sitting around the barbecue table or kicking back with a quiet few out on the deck. Adam scratched his stubbled chin. Perhaps they were in denial?

They weren't:

"We've been praying every day, son," confided Reg, as Adam escorted them to the elevator. "We'll be going to an extra mass this Easter as well."

"Thanks, Dad."

"The grandparents have been getting a workout, too."

Adam laughed. The 'grandparents'—the Blessed Virgin Mary and Joseph, her Most Chaste Spouse—occupied a pair of faded portrait prints, either side of the O'Doherty family photo in the folks' lounge room.

"Perhaps *you* should say a little prayer, Adam," suggested Eileen. "It wouldn't hurt to have a chat with the Almighty. Mention that a wonderful girl named Maddy is in need of a bit of extra TLC."

Adam pressed the 'Down' button and the elevator doors slid open. He gave his mother a kiss on the cheek as she stepped forward.

"I'll see what I can do."

*

There was a single message on the answering machine at home:

"Hi Ad—it's Shell here. I'm looking to dropping by Galbraith tomorrow if it's okay. Mum and Dad said Maddy was taking visitors. That's a good sign, isn't it? She must be feeling a little bit better about everything. The doctor she's got must be excellent. Quite a job to turn Maddy around after what you guys have experienced. Good thing, too—I don't want Magic Mad hating me when I get out of uni! Okay, I'll see you around six."

*

From: "Tin Lid" <womb@almighty.com>
To: "Adam O'Doherty" <edam_odoh@fathertobe.com>
Subject: Another Lesson

I still can't chill over Mum.

She hasn't said a word to me for days. When she talks to other people, the hollow heartbeat pounds every sentence. You reckon she is being extra protective, but I don't feel any safer. I feel buried.

Do you and Aunty Shelley feel that way, too? There was so much dark energy during her visit. Not even Sam could lighten things up. In fact, her being there seemed to be a big part of the problem.

Dad, you've already come through with a lesson in trust, so I will fight hard to nix the fear that Mum may never be the same again.

*

From: "Adam O'Doherty" <edam_odoh@fathertobe.com>
To: "Tin Lid" <womb@almighty.com>
Subject: Re: Another Lesson

Yes, Doctor Pole was central to the quite considerable tension of this evening. No fault of hers, though. The concerns stemmed from the message that Dawn Marks was unable to attend her check-in appointment...

*

"What's the hassle?" asked Shell. "Doctor Pole's here. She's your patient, isn't she, Doctor Pole?"

"Yes, she is."

"It's a little bit complicated, Shell," said Adam, knowing full well it wasn't complicated in the least.

Maddy raised her head. For the previous five minutes, she'd stared at her lap, picking at the double-stitch in her hospital issue blanket.

"I have not had a doctor examine me in the three weeks I've been here," she said evenly. "I'm not going to change that now. Not for anything or anyone. The hospital can kick me out if they want to, but they better be quick 'cause I'm ready to walk out on my own."

Silence reigned, save an announcement over the PA for an Orderly's required attendance in 7B. Adam rubbed the back of his neck before kneeling bedside on one knee. Sam fingered the small gold cross hanging from a chain around her neck. Michelle, eyebrows cocked and hands open, stared at each person in turn before settling on her brother.

"What do *you* want, bro? This is your child, too."

Adam looked toward Maddy, who had resumed her stitch-picking.

"I won't lie," he said. "I'd like Doctor Pole to do a check-up. She deserves our trust with the expertise she's demonstrated...and I'm not talking about the medical side of it. I think there's an opportunity here for us to learn trust."

Michelle advanced several steps. "It *is* an opportunity, Maddy! I know what you've been through now and I can definitely see how you might be...reluctant to have anything to do with doctors, particularly after that last arsehole took a piece of you and sent you on your way. But you must realise this is different. It's not unreasonable in this situation---"

"Sis?"

"What?"

"Shut up...please."

Adam claimed Maddy's hand. There was resistance at first—the limb seeking to join its companion in the customary shared position across the abdomen—then compliance.

"Yes, I'd like Doctor Pole to do a check-up," he said, "but I'm not the one receiving it, am I? I'm not the one laying in this bed. I'm not the one who's had to lie in beds like this before. I'm not the one having to fend off History whilst providing the life cord to our child. No, I'm not the one burdened with all that. God willing Shell, you and Doctor Pole will never be burdened with that either."

He got down on both knees.

"I have faith in you, babe. I believe in you. So does your child."

*

From: "Adam O'Doherty" <edam_odoh@fathertobe.com>
To: "Tin Lid" <womb@almighty.com>
Subject: Re: Another Lesson

...At this time Doctor Pole touched my shoulder, drawing me to standing. She retrieved the remote control from the tray and offered it to me, her face suggesting I understood what was required. I stabbed the 'On' button. The 'Neighbours' theme wafted out of the tube and hung in the hospital-issue air.

She then proposed a brief meeting with Shell and I in the hallway...

*

Samantha Pole extended a hand.

"Thank you for taking good care of my patient in there."

Adam hesitated, then accepted. Sam adjusted the hairclip holding her frizzy, burgundy tresses in place.

"I fell pregnant to my partner last year," she began. "We weren't trying at the time, so it was a bit of a shock, especially for a gynaecologist who's supposed to have some knowledge of these matters! But we were pleased. We took the attitude that we never really would be fully prepared to become parents anyway, so now was as good a time as ever."

Hospital traffic bustled all around the trio. A nurse corralled an old man wearing a dressing gown and using a Zimmer frame. A cleaner in a purple tunic whizzed by, his trolley of implements and supplies rattling like a 1950s train.

A solemn young man asked reception for the room number of his uncle. Adam and Michelle remained transfixed by the doctor's recount.

"It wasn't long before I knew something was wrong. I didn't realise the 'something' was an ectopic pregnancy until it was too late. It ruptured my fallopian tube at around 9pm on June 12th. We went straight to Emergency here at Galbraith and I was in surgery within the hour. They found close to a litre of blood in my abdomen. They also discovered that, for some unknown reason, the rupture had clotted so that the blood loss wasn't nearly as bad as it could have been. That unlikely little clot saved my life. I consider it my own personal miracle to this day."

Sam tucked her gold cross back under the collar of her shirt and dabbed her eyes with a tissue from her coat pocket. She cleared her throat then continued:

"Of course the tube was irreparable. Which means I've now only got half my original fertility. It also means we're living with the 'ectopic one-third rule': one-third chance of miscarriage, one-third chance of another ectopic, one-third chance of a normal pregnancy. These days, we *are* trying to get pregnant. I try to remember that even though we are in more difficult circumstances than we ever imagined there are others who've done it tougher." She glanced in the direction of the closed door to Maddy's room. "Others who've been burdened with more than what we're carrying. And in the end I figure, well, if I was good enough for one miracle, then maybe I'm good enough for two."

Her attention diverted to Michelle.

"Maddy has told me that you've been accepted into Medicine and you want to specialise in obstetrics."

Shell nodded. Sam smiled and narrowed her blue-eyed gaze.

"You're going to go okay. Keep in mind that not all the answers are in the textbooks."

She shifted her attention to the younger brother. Her voice took on the considered, clinical tone Adam recognised.

"Maddy informed me that the spotting has not appeared now for four days. She's experiencing no pain or discomfort and Dawn Marks' exam two days ago indicated the baby's vitals were fine. Provided she takes things nice and gentle, I think she can go home tomorrow." She handed over a business card. "That has my e-mail address on it. Stay in touch."

Adam held the card between the palms of his joined hands.

"Thank you. We will."

*

From: "Adam O'Doherty" <edam_odoh@fathertobe.com>
To: "Tin Lid" <womb@almighty.com>
Subject: Re: Another Lesson

...Mum can now see the end of this ordeal, B. That fact, and the small surprise I'm preparing for her return home, will mark the beginning of her journey back to the person we know and love.

Trust me.

*

The Intensive Care ward was calm; the usual buzz beyond her closed door, occasionally punctuated by a 'code blue' crescendo, had taken a rare breather. Tepid moonlight from the eastern window bathed the room in the palest of washes. The cavernous spaces reserved for life-saving machines contained a single packed, ready-to-go overnight suitcase and a single packed, ready-to-go rucksack.

Maddy rolled onto her side. Sleep was elusive, in part because of her imminent---

(victory)

---departure, the remainder due to the evening's episode. A particular statement from Michelle had left a sting she was finding difficult to shake off:

"What do *you* want bro? This is your child, too."

From the time she'd arrived at the hospital, everything had been about her, about what *she* wanted. Was that unreasonable? Throughout the three weeks, she had remained steadfast in those wants and the result was, for the first time in six years, she was walking out of the hospital still pregnant. Did such a result justify the flagrant disregard of her husband's wishes?

"I guess we'll find out in the morning, Kiddo," she whispered.

*

Adam unlocked the front door to 150 James Street and led a blindfolded Maddy across the threshold.

"Kiddo, tell me what's going on!" she cried.

Adam raised an index finger to his lips. "Don't say a word."

He manouevred Maddy in behind the couch and placed her hands on the backrest.

"What's this stuff?"

"Take off the blindfold and have a look."

Maddy removed the bandana and observed a living room quite unlike the one she'd been whisked away from twenty-three days before. Streamers and balloons hung from the ceiling, the furniture, and the gently rotating fan above. A laminated banner on the wall above the TV read: "OUT OF BED…FULL STEAM AHEAD!!!". Gifts jostled for space on the coffee table. Adam pressed the remote for the stereo. As the funky upper cuts of John Butler Trio's 'Zebra' weighed in, a bemused Maddy stroked a section of the Mintie and Mars bar wrappers adorning the couch.

"The pressies are from our friends," said Adam. "The framed photo of you standing next to the Big Pineapple is from the folks and Chris. The baby sling is from Jay-Jay and Boyd—apparently there were two of them in that Expo hamper. Ah, the book is from Kelly and Sandy."

Maddy examined the cover. "*Secrets of the Baby*

Whisperer?"

"Comes highly recommended. They also provided the muffins. The stuffed cow is from Dilip Shastrani at school. He says in India, good luck is assured with a new baby or with a new cow. He reckons with both we're laughing. What else have we got? The dozen white roses are from-"

"Michelle."

Adam paused, noting his wife's half-smile. "That's right. The chrysanthemums are from Doctor Pole and those brochures must have been left in the mailbox by the Mormons. And this---" He moved toward her, wound his left arm around her shoulders, cradled the back of her head in his right hand and held her, gently rocking side to side, "---that's from Canada."

"And what do I get from you, Sir Fix-A-Lot?" inquired Maddy, burying her head deeper into his chest.

Adam laughed. "For starters – a decent bloody omelette!" He kissed his wife's forehead and made to leave. Maddy held his hand, delaying his departure.

"I'm sorry, gorgeous handsome man. For being…for everything."

Adam placed a hand against her tummy.

"We're glad to have you back."

14

From: "Adam O'Doherty" <edam_odoh@fathertobe.com>
To: "Tin Lid" <womb@almighty.com>
Subject: Closer Still

Another e-mail from Tristan—another two rejections. Kendrick & Sons was one of them. Tristan assured me it's all good and that their turn down had nothing to do with the work, but rather with the fact that they recently had a huge overhaul of staff and didn't want to take on anyone else at this time. He thought I had a strong chance with them, and I must confess I thought I had a strong chance with them, too. They were ranked second on my 'Make Adam O'Doherty a Star' chart, second only to Hutton House.

I realise now, however, that this could not have been any other way. A green light from Kendrick & Sons at this time would've been disastrous. It would've distracted my focus away from Maddy in her hour of need. Sure it would've been the dream come true, but could celebration and pride be justified with your wife lying in a hospital bed?

A deal with Hutton House is obviously the masterplan's intention. Their Editor-In-Charge knows me, knows Tristan, knows the work. They liked what they saw in the first two submissions and they are actively and aggressively marketing new writers. Tristan has said from day one that Hutton House was a 'gimme' and that shopping it around the other bigs was really just to 'test the water, swim with the sharks, see if we can catch a bigger fish to fry'.

So there weren't any other bites? Well let's cook up the one already in the boat.

Bring on Destiny.

I'm ready now.

A Life More Ordinary

15

From: "Adam O'Doherty" <edam_odoh@fathertobe.com>
To: "Tin Lid" <womb@almighty.com>
Subject: Share The Wealth Around

Your 'helper' is certainly generous, B.

It seems Destiny can accommodate a modicum of dream fulfillment beyond the O'Dohertys of New Farm. So many of the people around us right now are receiving a nod and a wink in the direction of desires long held.

For others, desires not so long held...

*

Adam held his hand over the receiver.

"Maddy…call. It's Jenna. She wants to talk to you. She says it's important."

He handed the phone over and stood by. Maddy noticed his continued presence after the initial 'hello'.

"You can go now," she said, flicking her fingers.

Adam retreated to the kitchen and feigned washing the dishes. Hell must have frozen over, he thought. The great hoax is about to end.

It had taken a toll on Jay-Jay he could hardly fathom. Her guilt, though thoroughly misguided, had been real enough to affect her health. She'd missed the first two days of second term and another the following week. At school, she'd appeared so listless and harried, so unlike her usual bouncing-ball self, that Adam had approached her insisting, pleading, begging he tell Maddy.

"That won't be necessary," had been her only response.

After two and a half months, it certainly *seemed* necessary. He had held his tongue, though, and now, at last, his best teaching buddy could go back to being the 'High School Sweetheart' instead of the 'High School Dropout'.

Adam crept closer to the kitchen entrance and was nearly bowled over by a fridge-focused Maddy barreling through.

"You're wanted on the phone now," she said, extracting a pair of stray chicken drumsticks from the crisper and holding them up like semaphore flags.

"What did she say?"

"Do you have to know?"

"Yes! I have to know."

Maddy bit into one of the legs and spoke after several chews: "We're gonna try and get into the same ante-natal class."

Adam strode over to the wall shelf in the hallway and snatched up the waiting cordless.

"Jay-Jay, for cryin' out loud-"

"It's Boyd."

"Ah...good. Maybe you can talk some sense into her. This has got to stop!"

Boyd laughed. "Can't stop it now, mate."

"What, are you just going to let this charade keep going until she's being wheeled into the delivery room? Or are you stalling so you can *actually* get her pregnant?"

"Wrong tense on 'get', mate. It's 'got'."

"What?"

"'Got'. 'Got' her pregnant. She *is* actually pregnant."

Adam held the phone out at arm's length, tapped it against the wall shelf and brought it back to his ear.

"Jay-Jay is pregnant."

"She is."

"She's with child."

"Uh-huh."

"To her husband."

"I hope so, yes."

Adam lowered his voice. "Does Maddy know?"

"Of course she bloody knows, you goose!"

Adam scrunched his eyes shut and shook his head. "I have to sit down." He drifted into the lounge room, flopped down into the recliner and levered the footrest into position. "How the Christ did this happen?"

"Standard procedure. No turkey basters required."

"*When* did this happen?"

"Hang on a sec." Boyd's voice became distant. "Hey, Jenna! Adam would like to know *when* this happened?" A stifled groan coursed down the line. "As far as we can tell," resumed Boyd, "it probably happened *the night she said it happened*!"

"No way!"

"Do you remember the storm, and me saying we had to make the most of the blackout? I think we did."

Adam got up and walked into the spare room. Its transformation into a nursery was in full swing. The bookshelf had been relocated, so too the box of Maddy's snorkeling equipment. The wardrobe that stored their winter woolies was gone, replaced by a chest of drawers with teddy-bear trim. An Anne Geddes picture of a potted child/chili plant hung where a poster of Einstein had once resided. The computer remained—it would be the last to go.

"How do you guys feel? This mucks up your seven year plan, doesn't it?"

Boyd exhaled. "Yeah, it does a bit. But that's usually how it is with plans, isn't it? They don't necessarily go the way you expect them to go. I think it was really more *my* plan anyway. Jen may have talked up not wanting a kid in the past—'Who'd want to bring a child into a world of war and hunger and cloning and endless Survivor series...' and all the rest of it. But I don't think she fooled anyone. She's never been happier, I can tell you right now." He snorted. "Of course, I'm a different story! I just about shat myself when I found out. But now the dust has settled a bit, I'm really settling into the idea of being a Dad. In fact I can't wait!"

"Good on you, Boyd."

"Who would've thunk it, hey? The Boss upstairs works in mysterious ways."

*

From: "Adam O'Doherty" <edam_odoh@fathertobe.com>
To: "Tin Lid" <womb@almighty.com>
Subject: Share The Wealth Around

...Add to that piece of unlikely synergy the following:

Shelley has just begun her Medicine studies (she says there's lots of textbooks, she's starting late, but she believes she's already one lesson up on the rest of the group)

Reg and Eileen are buying out entire baby shops and thumbing their noses at friends with grandkids.

Chris had a second date last night.

Kelly babysat one of his chiropractic client's children last weekend and returned the very same child—clean, undamaged and unbandaged—into their care.

It's not just the home front providing these wondrous turns. School is getting its fair share, too. And the trend has not gone unnoticed by a certain wise man of my acquaintance...

*

"We have a saying in India: 'Good fortune is a better procreator than the most virile of men'." Dilip ceased his scrutiny of Jenna's Q and A crowd at the far end of the lunch table and addressed Adam. "Have you heard the other big news?"

"No."

"Cal's leaving."

Adam's fork paused in its twirl of last night's leftover spaghetti bolognaise. "You're kidding."

"Not at all. He's going via the 'Different Employment' scheme"

"The 'Deadwood Fifty Grand'? I thought he didn't apply for that."

"So he said. He must have changed his mind at the last

moment. Good thing he did."

"The lifer's getting a new life—how about that?"

Adam peeked over his shoulder in the direction of Callum Morecroft's desk. The Carsmair veteran was sitting alone, elbows propped on two piles of unfinished reports, munching on a ham and salad roll. The look on his face suggested he would soon be joined by Donald Trump. Upon completion of the paperwork, the tycoon would inform everyone bar the Deadwood beneficiary that they were fired.

"Do you know what he's using the money for?"

Dilip took up an imaginary waltz partner. "I believe he wants to run a dance studio."

"What?"

"It's something he's always wanted to do apparently. I've been told he's quite the mover."

"And he never let on. The old dog!"

"His daughter is going to work with him."

"Lots of people wanting pole dancing lessons, hey?"

"I think she's sticking to Latin and Ballroom."

Adam wiped his mouth with a paper towel. "Well, that is undoubtedly big news."

Dilip grinned and suggestively swayed his hips. "Yes, but good fortune is not yet prepared for the after-cigarette, my friend! Did you hear about The Sarge's excitement? For the first time this Anzac Day, he will be able to march with four generations of his family. And then there's the Carsmair senior girls' hockey team making the state finals, and the performance group winning the Rock Eisteddfod. Rahul Dravid, my favourite batsman, scored a century on the weekend! Here, look at the paper."

Adam scanned the front page. "So, we were the first allies to commit troops to the war, hey? The Prime Minister of Australia is, officially, the American President's lapdog."

"You see? Even our head of state is Good Fortune's mistress. And now he is living his dream!" Dilip rubbed his hands together. "All this promiscuity bodes very well for a great writer awaiting the fruits of his labour. You think?"

Adam scooped the last of the spaghetti sauce with his index finger then held it skyward.

"We have a saying in Australia, Dee: 'Bloody oath!'"

*

From: "Adam O'Doherty" <edam_odoh@fathertobe.com>
To: "Tin Lid" <womb@almighty.com>
Subject: Share The Wealth Around

...As I conclude this e-mail, the master copy of *The Ordinary Man's Enemy* sits at my left elbow.

In this form, it presents a mirage of susceptibility to its predecessors' fate. Big, bulky and held together by a bland yellow A4 wallet, it could easily substitute for any one of the failures stashed away in storage. As a plain old manuscript, it appears to hold no more promise of deliverance than a positive pregnancy test.

I can't wait to see it transformed into a book. To hold it in my hands when it is delivered into the world.

Confirmation from Hutton House should arrive this week.

16

Adam stood in the centre of the lounge room. The choking heat of a throwback-to-summer day filled his every pore. His shirt clung to his back. Sweat dripped from his brow, the beads smudging the letterhead of the paper in his hand. The ceiling fan, operating at its highest speed, carved the fug without providing respite. Cars thumped and bumped over the traffic calming on James Street.

It was the 29th April, 2003.

It was a life-changing day.

Adam sat down on the couch. He placed the letter on a nearby cushion. He picked up the stereo remote from the coffee table and pressed 'Off', silencing Hunters and Collectors' 'Newborn' mid-chorus. He placed the remote on top of the letter and leaned back.

His head was a haze. Eyes, able to see far into the future five minutes earlier, could scarcely focus on the furniture. His chest was filling up with sandbags, crowding in on his fragile heart. His stomach burned. Bile stained his throat.

"God," he croaked. "What more?"

Adam slid down off the couch and onto his haunches. Arms wrapped around his midriff, he bent forward until his forehead pressed down onto the polished timber floor.

*

"What did it say?"

A prostrate Adam glanced at his wife. She was seated at the foot of the couch, arms wrapped around his bent knees, swollen tummy against his shins, cheek against the backrest.

"Does it really matter, Mad?" He felt her pat his thigh and checked himself. "Tristan said they thought it was great, but when it came to a decision about whether to commission the work or not, they felt it would be better written…as a TV series."

"Oh no."

"Oh yes. 'It's all good if you'd like to take it in a different direction', he said. But as for his continuing to act as agent, he felt there wasn't any more he could do. And if there *was* anything more to be done, best that it be done by somebody who could put in the sort of time and energy the work deserved."

"You?"

"Me."

"Bastard."

Adam wiped his nose with the back of his hand. "You know what's the worst thing about this, the thing I just can't get my head around? *The Ordinary Man's Enemy* could not have had any more in its favour, Mad. Every base was covered. It had been evaluated. It had been plugged. The publisher had requested more of it be sent. It attracted an agent---"

"Bastard."

"---with a noted name and client list. The work was polished, praised and earmarked for really good things. Nothing was left to chance. And it still came up short."

Maddy moved down and off the couch. She sat cross-legged on the floor and held her husband's hand as if preparing for an arm wrestle.

"It didn't come up short," she said. "It got you further than you ever were before. The next one will go further still."

Adam scoffed. "The next one? What next one?"

"*The* next one. You've been into it the last few months. Haven't you?"

"No, that's not a story. It's something…it's something different."

Maddy drummed the fingernails of her free hand on the armrest then shrugged. "Well, whether you do a new story right now or in ten years time, the fact is you can't *not* do the next one. Writing is your gift and it's your necessity. It's like breathing for you."

"In that case, I need mouth-to-mouth."

Adam extended his legs. His feet found the still-present grooves created by 'Modified Bed Rest'.

"I've got nothing, babe. No ideas, no inclination...and now no reason."

*

From: "Tin Lid" <womb@almighty.com>
To: "Adam O'Doherty" <edam_odoh@fathertobe.com>
Subject: Yes Reason

Yo Dad

Aren't you one more rejection closer to your triumph?

*

From: "Adam O'Doherty" <edam_odoh@fathertobe.com>
To: "Tin Lid" <womb@almighty.com>
Subject: Re: Yes Reason

B

Real life is very different from the bravado of writers. Real life doesn't always have room for everyone's dreams.

The umpire's decision is final. I now have to work my way towards accepting that decision.

*

Kelly ducked as the speeding tennis ball flew towards his head. It grazed his scalp (he would later claim to have lost an extra millimetre from his buzz-cut) and crashed into the back netting on the full.

"So you're coming to terms with the disappointment then, Ed."

Adam banged the soles of his sneakers with the racquet frame. "It's a joke, Kel! A fucking joke! They wouldn't know talent if it stuffed a rejection letter up their arse!" He moved to the backhand court and, without taking time or aim, slammed down a serve. It pinged off the net post and into the adjoining court. "It's all about money and nothing to do with art. They'll publish the local weather-girl's bloody life story, even though she can't write for shit! They'll bang off five hundred thousand copies and paste her mug on billboards all over the city! Why? Because she's got a sliver of celebrity, that's why. And the poor bastards who've got real writing talent but didn't get on 'Big Brother'...well they can go screw themselves."

"Real talent can't be squashed forever, Ed," countered Kelly, leaving court to retrieve the wayward ball. "And you *have* got real talent—jeez, even a newspaper reading back-cracker like me can see that. It'll find its way into the spotlight." He lobbed the Spalding to his partner, hoping to initiate a gentle, soothing, soul-searching rally.

Adam whacked it into the carpark.

"How?" he shouted. "Tell me how it'll find its way into the spotlight? I've got a kid on the way, a wife who wants to stay at home with the kid, a mortgage, car loan, credit card debts—that's the definition of a public servant! I'm gonna be a teacher for the rest of my life, pal. Name me one teacher who's made a name for themselves in a creative industry?"

"Gene Simmons from 'Kiss'."

"It's useless! No time to write when you're a public servant, sole provider and Super-Dad, Kel. No time to indulge dreams when pragmatism's got you by the short and curlies."

Kelly crossed the net and jogged for the exit. "Don't get so riled that you give it away, man. Don't let those---"

*

"---mongrels have the satisfaction again." Jenna pulled her strapless shoulders back and cast an eye over the sixty or so guests present for Callum Morecroft's send-off. "You will end up leaving in style, Ad, but not if you grovel at the feet of those...mongrels."

Adam swayed, handed his drink—a White Russian—to Boyd and laid both hands on his pregnant friend's shoulders.

"Gimme your mobile, Shweetheart."

"No. I won't let you make a dick of yourself."

He turned to Boyd. "Gimme yoursh then."

"Don't do it," warned Jenna.

Boyd emptied his pockets. "Can't help you, champ," he said. "And even if I could I wouldn't. Jen's right: you don't want to suck up to the people that gave you a bollocking."

Adam turned to Dilip. The Indian held a hand up, preventing a third slurred request. Adam retrieved his drink from Boyd and sat heavily in a nearby chair.

"I *could* convince them to take me, you know. I *could* make them like me. I could take five percent royaltiesh, or pay for some of the marketing shtuff outta my own pocket." Adam emptied the glass and tinkled the leftover ice. "I'd shign the shittiest contract they could poshibly give me and I wouldn't complain...just ash long ash they gave me a book."

Jenna grabbed the lapels of Adam's jacket, thought better of shaking some sense into an already addled brain, then addressed Dilip:

"Isn't there something meaningful you can say to him?"

Dilip fronted his man, eye to glassy eye.

"We have a saying in India: 'A man who drinks too many White Russians will end up thinking---"

*

"---long-service leave is not a bad thing. Tell him, Reginald. Tell him coming up to ten years as a teacher in May doesn't mean he can never write another story."

Reg gave a calming flute of champagne to Eileen and scooped a mound of cabbage into the peanut satay goulash.

"You've got a good job, son. You'd be a fool to toss it in." A withering glare from Eileen prompted a hasty qualification. "Because it can help your writing, I mean! You'd be a fool to toss it in because it can help with your writing! Long-service leave could be used to knock up a new book!"

Adam continued tracing around a cork placemat with his finger.

"You could be a whole lot worse off, Adam," offered Chris, ducking low toward the table, trying to catch his older brother's eye. "There are plenty of would-be artists working jobs that aren't nine to three. And don't get on your high horse telling me teachers work eight 'til eight—I know some of 'em do and I know you're not one of them. Plenty of those would-be artists don't get ten weeks a year holiday either, just quietly."

Adam sighed and shifted his auto-obsessive routine to the salt and pepper shakers.

"The future is still yours to shape, brud," assured Shell. "So let's make it interesting, shall we? Let's have a new race. Your first book up against my first episiotomy? What do you say?"

Adam folded his arms and stared at the Lladro porcelain clown on the mantel.

"Can you contribute something to this, Woody?" asked Eileen.

The border collie leapt to his feet, scampered under the table and planted his slobbering features in the crotch of the commanded target. The visiting master remained motionless.

"I'm afraid we've done all we can, team," declared Michelle, returning to her bookmarked page of 'Grey's Anatomy'. "Looks like a terminal case of feeling sorry for---"

*

"---the way you've been feeling and behaving the last fortnight…maybe you should give this first class a miss."

Adam lifted the printed sheets out of the tray. The heading at the top of each sheet read: 'Ante-Natal Notes—Week One'. He tucked them into a bland yellow A4 wallet already containing three pencils, an eraser and a highlighter.

"I'm a lot better now, Maddy."

"Better?"

"Relieved actually. I didn't realise how much of a burden writing had become."

"Transforming your own unique thoughts and ideas into wonderful words…that was a burden?"

Adam began stuffing the master copy of *The Ordinary Man's Enemy* into a plastic shopping bag. "No. No, that was never a burden. All the other stuff was. The collating, the posting, the spruiking. The waiting. The problem was all that stuff far outweighed the magic."

"That stuff had a purpose, Adam." Maddy observed the bag handles being tied. "You're not throwing your story away are you?"

"I'm just going to put it in the garage with the others."

"Give it to me."

"Maddy."

"*Give* it to me."

Adam handed the bagged manuscript over. Maddy held it to her belly.

"That stuff had a purpose," she repeated. "It was meant to create more opportunities for you to make magic. It was meant to have magic become the thing you made most often."

"Well, it didn't work out that way, did it?"

Adam picked up the yellow wallet and crossed the floor of the spare room. At the threshold of the door, he banged the butt of his fist into the jamb and pivoted back toward his wife.

"I'm trying to accept this now and move on. Why can't you?"

Maddy smoothed the plastic bag, allowing the title page of the abandoned novel to show through.

"Because I'd be failing you if I did."

17

From: "Tin Lid" <womb@almighty.com>
To: "Adam O'Doherty" <edam_odoh@fathertobe.com>
Subject: Acceptance

Dad

That place we went to tonight was tops. Right from the beginning, I felt the same sort of buzz that Mum gets when she goes shopping for bigger pants...

*

"Good evening, everyone and welcome to this six week antenatal course. My name is Dawn Marks. For those people who don't know me—and looking around I think I know almost all of you—yes, I am from New Zealand. I had intended to teach you all the 'Haka' to get you in the mindset for what lays ahead, particularly as regards labour, but I think we might give that one a miss! I was thinking we might start by going around the room. Just tell us your names, your due dates—Dads, you can tell those!—and a few details about the finding out you were pregnant. Just a little bit on the how, when and where. Josh and Margie...how about you start?"

*

From: "Tin Lid" <womb@almighty.com>
To: "Adam O'Doherty" <edam_odoh@fathertobe.com>
Subject: Acceptance

...You seemed cool about things. More than you have been for a while...

*

Adam chuckled as Lynette and Boris Pfaff—the third couple to speak—re-enacted the 7-11 fainting scene in their pregnancy revelation.

This is magic, he thought. Magic that could never be outweighed by the burden.

He had no clue how the Pfaffs had arrived at this moment. Perhaps theirs was an instant success story, not unlike the especial Grimsons, seated in the two chairs beside his own. Wham, bam, thank you *pram*! Or perhaps the Pfaffs had battled History themselves? It was possible—they were the far side of thirty-something and this was their first child. Perhaps they had worn experiences that he and Maddy could never have imagined, not even in the coldest, cruelest prisons of their six-year despair? If that was indeed the background of Lynette and Boris Pfaff, did they then view the scales of worth as tipped toward the sublime?

Judging from their animated thank you's and playful kisses, the answer was a definitive 'Yes'.

Adam applauded with the rest of the group, threw in a whistle for good measure. More opportunities for him to make magic, to have magic become the thing he made most often: that was what Maddy wanted for him? Well, just as surely as a miracle correspondence pointed the way at home, the promise of magic was right here in this room.

A child.

Truly, the ultimate vehicle to rise above the mundane.

There would be burdens of course—every parent endured them and Adam O'Doherty would be no exception. 'The Umbilical Word' was proof enough of that, too. But, in the end, how would the trials stack up against the triumph?

They wouldn't. And you couldn't ask for more out of life than that.

Destiny's finally arrived, he thought.

What a story.

*

"Thanks Rosie and Paul…found out in a port-a-loo at the rodeo, wow. Fitting after a roll in the hay. Okay, next up… Jenna? Boyd?"

The Grimsons whispered to themselves for a moment, then nodded.

"We'd like to stray from tradition for our recount if we may," said Jenna, rising to her feet. "We'd like our good friend Adam O'Doherty, who's here with his lovely pregnant wife Maddy, to tell our story. He was the reason we got pregnant *twice*."

Raised eyebrows accompanied cries of 'Wooooohhh'.

"Yes, it sounds rather weird, but he can explain. Over to you, Ad-"

"What are you doing, sweetheart?" asked Adam, pinching his friend's forearm.

Jenna leaned close. She spoke with a hand in front of her mouth, but at the same pitch as her previous statements.

"We can't do justice to it. A story like this needs a writer's voice."

Eyebrows sat high on foreheads once more.

"And, anyway, you've been busting to tell Maddy all about it for months now. Here's your chance."

Adam pivoted toward his wife. She was trying to suppress a grin.

"Let's hear it then," she said.

"Yes! Let's!" added Dawn, eyes larger than boiled eggs.

Adam rubbed the back of his neck then stood like a convicted man receiving sentence.

"Ladies, gentlemen…and former friends. This is a story of immaculate *mis*-conception…"

*

Maddy stared in amazement. The tale spinning from her Adam's lips was, to put it mildly, incredible. But it was not responsible for her awe.

It was the audience.

They'd fallen in love with her husband.

Mouths sat agape. Bodies leaned forward. Whispered comments out of turn brought impatient 'shooshes' from partners unwilling to miss a word. Entertaining stories had been the stock-in-trade of the class thus far, but it was the *telling* of this one that would later compel a sharing of it with friends, prefaced by the statement 'Wait till you hear this, it's a *classic*!'. Women with bladders the size of thimbles ignored the call of nature. Men with attention spans the duration of sports reports sat transfixed in the front half of their seats. Every sentence added to the adventure. Every punchline placed a stamp on the evening.

As the star resumed his seat and the newly won fans' applause commenced, Maddy reflected on how moments such as these should've constituted the norm. For so long now, and for the past six years in particular, Adam had been everything but what he could be. Teacher, husband, major income earner. Life-support. Time devoted to his dream—his *being* – amounted to little more than late night vigils and stolen moments. And now, confronted with a publication setback and impending fatherhood, he was prepared to forego even those meagre spoils.

It didn't have to be this way. Giving stories to the world was his calling, just as assuredly as becoming a mother was hers. And if this episode wasn't a convincing enough reminder of that truth, then there was really only one thing left to say.

*

From: "Tin Lid" <womb@almighty.com>
To: "Adam O'Doherty" <edam_odoh@fathertobe.com>
Subject: Acceptance

...Mum and you had a private sesh at one point. I couldn't understand everything, but I did notice a repeat of things spoken at the hospital...

*

Maddy turned and faced Adam. She took his hand and cleared her throat with a small cough.

"I'm sorry, babe," he said, pulling a flinched face and pre-empting her strike. "Jay-Jay wanted to tell you so many times but-"

"Tut-tut." Maddy put her free hand over his mouth. "Listen to me—this is important."

She stared deep into the eyes of the man who'd courted her with handwritten love poems written on the back of 'Aldous Huxley' lesson plans.

"I won't lie," she said. "I'd like you to create more stories and give them a chance to fly. You deserve some self-trust with the expertise you've demonstrated...and, yes, I'm talking about the events of tonight. I think there's an opportunity here for you to learn self-trust."

"Maddy, look. Don't do this. It's not necessar-"

"Adam?"

"What?"

"Shut up...please."

Maddy got down on both knees. A mortified Adam glanced around to see if their hallway cubby-hole had attracted any spectators. There were none.

"Yes, my husband, I'd like to see another story get the chance of making a dream come true...but I'm not the one writing it, am I? I'm not the one risking rejection letters. I'm not the one who's had to wear rejection letters in the past. I'm not the one having to fend off History whilst providing the life cord to a dream. No, I'm not the one burdened with all that."

Maddy stood once more, raised her shirt several inches and placed Adam's hand on her bare abdomen.

"I have faith in you, babe. I believe in you."

Adam's mouth moved soundlessly up and down. His eyes rivalled those of the midwife currently calling for an end to the intermission and a resumption of class.

"God Almighty," he blurted. "There's kicks! I can feel *kicks*!"

Maddy lowered her shirt and smiled.

"I believe in you…and so does your child."

*

From: "Tin Lid" <womb@almighty.com>
To: "Adam O'Doherty" <edam_odoh@fathertobe.com>
Subject: Acceptance

...So are you still determined to bail out on your dream? Or do we need to weep and wail and gnash teeth (gums in my case) in addition to getting down on the knees?

18

From: "Adam O'Doherty" <edam_odoh@fathertobe.com>
To: "Tin Lid" <womb@almighty.com>
Subject: Re: Acceptance

Your mother (and you) can put away the self-flagellation until you're a teenager—I've decided to give the umpire one last chance at getting it right.

Should be a swift decision, too. A ready-made story idea was available to me all along. Now it will be sent out into the world before you can say 'Howzat!'

'Make it or die trying,' as the saying goes....

*

From: "Tin Lid" <womb@almighty.com>
To: "Adam O'Doherty" <edam_odoh@fathertobe.com>
Subject: Acceptance

Wicked!

And don't be afraid, Dad. The Great Gonzo here reckons **it's better to die trying than to die wondering.**

Letters to Limbo

19

From: "Adam O'Doherty" <edam_odoh@fathertobe.com>
To: "Tin Lid" <womb@almighty.com>
Subject: Ohmigod

Dearest B

I got an unexpected phone call an hour ago...

*

"Adam speaking."

"Adam…James Fox, Hutton House Publishers."

"Who?"

"James Fox. Editor-in-Charge at Hutton House. How are you?"

Maddy stepped out of the bathroom, crooning the chorus of Red Hot Chili Peppers' 'Scar Tissue'. Upon seeing Adam, she mouthed the words 'Who is it?' Adam rolled his eyes.

"James Fox, is it?" he replied.

"Yes."

"From Hutton House."

"Yes."

"A-ha."

Adam swigged from the bottle of Spring Valley apple juice in his left hand, sloshed it around, swallowed, leaked an exaggerated 'Aaahhh'.

"You suck, Kel."

"Kel?"

"Don't think you're gonna be spending time with our kid if you behave like this."

The cad's voice muffled for a moment, engaging in some palm-over-the-receiver Plan B with a fellow conspirator, no doubt Sandy. Adam swirled the sediment in his drink.

"Kel..." resumed the caller. "Is that the one you called 'Kelvin' in your submission?"

Swirling became plummeting. Sediment mingled with broken glass on the floor.

"It's not...Jenna...is it?"

"The faker? No."

"Nor anyone else who might be taking the mickey."

"Not today."

"It is James then."

"Yes."

"James Fox."

"Yes."

"Of Hutton House."

A burbling laugh trickled down the line.

"Would you prefer to do this by e-mail, Adam?"

*

From: "Adam O'Doherty" <edam_odoh@fathertobe.com>
To: "Tin Lid" <womb@almighty.com>
Subject: Ohmigod

...They want it, B! They want US!

THEY WANT THE UMBILICAL WORD!

I sent away a few of our early correspondences (names altered to protect the innocent) and a sketchy book proposal giving an idea as to how it might hang together, 'Contemporary comic fable about chasing dreams, confronting loss, finding your destiny', yada yada etcetera etcetera.

THEY LOVE IT!

They want to send a contract out straight away and get an editor working on what I've got so far. Jim (he said that's what his friends called him) asked if I had sent this elsewhere and I told him, truthfully, that I hadn't. He was quite relieved. He thinks other publishers would be very interested in this work. He reckons *The Umbilical Word* could be 'hot property'.

I am stunned. Beyond stunned. As I sit here at the computer, my fingers are tingling so much I can hardly type. Doctor Pole's words keep running through my mind: 'If I was good enough for one miracle, then maybe I'm good enough for two'.

Maddy is beside herself. When I told her the news, she repeated every word so that her 'Kiddo' could share in the moment (so this news is most likely no news to you). Then she rang her family in Canada who, because of a heightened stimulation in one of Tammy's chakras, were already waiting by the phone.

It's funny—I thought she might be a bit non-plussed because I had peddled our story without okaying it with her first...

*

"Are you kidding?"

Maddy leaned forward. The recliner gave way. Adam, lap supporting his wife's full bulk, fell back amidst a chorus of spring twangs and vinyl farts. The old Jason was a goner. Neither user cared.

"I think it's great, gorgeous handsome man."

"You do?"

"I'm thrilled my original idea has led to this. Well, actually, it was Professor Emmett G Bragg's idea originally, wasn't it?"

"The man's a genius."

"But I brought it to your attention, so you owe me big-time."

"I owe you everything, babe."

Maddy caressed her belly. Adam saw that her navel, after weeks of brave resistance, had finally popped. It now resembled a trumpet mute. It rendered Maddy's abdomen unrecognisable from the previous day. Amazing, he thought, how things could appear so very different so very quickly.

"I think sharing our experiences with the world will bring things full circle," Maddy said. "I think it will bring closure."

"Yes it will, Oprah," replied Adam, pulling his wife into a clumsy, squealy embrace.

*

From: "Adam O'Doherty" <edam_odoh@fathertobe.com>
To: "Tin Lid" <womb@almighty.com>
Subject: Ohmigod

...I need a drink.

Thank you for believing in me.

Look forward to your reply.

Dad

*

From: "Adam O'Doherty" <edam_odoh@fathertobe.com>
To: "Tin Lid" <womb@almighty.com>
Subject: Too Much

B

I signed the contract today. It was a surreal experience, even more so than the week preceding. The phone hasn't stopped ringing. Messages from friends, family, rellies, acquaintances...

Agents.

They all wanted to introduce themselves, touch base, let me know that they were here for me, that they were available at a time of my convenience to negotiate the best possible deal for me. Most of them rang twice. Tristan rang seven times. On the last occasion, I decided to put him out of his misery and pick up...

*

"Tristan."

"Oh, hi. Adam. Superb! Beginning to think you might've moved house or something."

"No, we're still right here, Tristan. Same phone number. Same postal address, too."

"Yes, okay. And how's Mandy?"

"Mandy is good."

"She's pregnant, isn't she, as per the character in your new masterpiece?"

"No, she's not. I made all that stuff up. She's actually

training for Circus Oz."

"Fabulous! What does she do?"

"She can hang hula-hoops off her belly button."

"That's quite a trick."

"Mmm."

"Quite a trick alright. A showstopper. Something to really break the ice at parties, too I imag-"

"Tristan."

"Yes, Adam."

"I'm a busy man."

"Yes, of course. Well...I just wanted to throw my hat in the ring, run my flag up the pole."

"Pardon?"

"You know...I'm...here for you Adam. I'm available at a time of your convenience to negotiate the best possible-"

"Tristan."

"Yes, Adam."

"It's all good."

"It is?"

"Yes. The new masterpiece is in the hands of someone who can put in the sort of time and energy the work deserves."

"Ah."

*

From: "Adam O'Doherty" <edam_odoh@fathertobe.com>
To: "Tin Lid" <womb@almighty.com>
Subject: Too Much

...Throughout the week, I couldn't get my head around the fact that Adam O'Doherty and *The Umbilical Word* were as the prophesy foretold—hot property! These people, these industry people, unreachable for the last ten years, were clamouring over each other to get to *me*! To get to *my work*!

And then the contract arrived.

Jim Fox delivered it personally. I gave it the once over and very nearly inscribed my name after Lynette and Boris Pfaff on the 'Faintheart' honour roll...

*

Adam looked up from the document.

"There's an advance."

Jim Fox stroked his grey goatee with the middle knuckles of his right hand and nodded.

"It's a healthy advance. Better than healthy."

"We feel it's money well spent."

Adam scanned the kitchen. His gaze came to rest upon his briefcase, bloated with tests and reports and a diary full of doodles, lying awkwardly in the space under the water purifier, untouched since its Friday abandonment.

"I'm going to be leaving school soon," he said, eyes returning to the set of papers that would christen a brand new, Italian leather briefcase in the week to come. "And I don't think I'll be going back."

Jim Fox removed his spectacles from the bridge of his nose and let them hang from the lanyard around his neck. He extended a hand.

"Let's make magic."

*

From: "Adam O'Doherty" <edam_odoh@fathertobe.com>
To: "Tin Lid" <womb@almighty.com>
Subject: Too Much

...I signed (my name, I think), shook hands, and waved goodbye to Hutton House's number one star-maker as he drove away from 150 James Street. Maddy felt my copy of the contract ought to be immortalised. She spent the afternoon hunting down a frame and, as I write these words, she is hanging it on the wall nearest the busted recliner.

This is all too much, little B. Contracts, advances, getting out of teaching. What is a man to do when the dream and reality meld as one?

I think I'll have another drink.

Still looking forward to your reply.

Dad

*

From: "Adam O'Doherty" <edam_odoh@fathertobe.com>
To: "Tin Lid" <womb@almighty.com>
Subject: Par-tay

B

You are probably aware that Mum and I have just attended a big celebratory bash at my parents' house. Everyone was there, even Doctor Pole. There were lots of highlights. For my personal fave, I couldn't split Kel's hyperactive karaoke of Midnight Oil's 'King of the Mountain' and Reg's toast with the 'Wally Lewis Testimonial' port.

All through the evening, people were asking me if the lost pregnancy stuff in the story was, in truth, really about us...

*

Adam surveyed the pressing faces. Jenna held her interlocked hands at her breast. Boyd tapped his index finger against his lips. Dilip's undeniable smile suggested he already possessed the truth and that his friend's answer was immaterial.

"I write fiction, guys," replied Adam. "It's a made-up couple."

"No way!" cried Jenna.

"Way."

"But those experiences—you don't just pull those out of thin air. You and Maddy must have been through something similar. At least."

Adam brushed an invisible piece of lint from his collar. "What does it matter, Jay?"

"What *does* it matter?" seconded Dilip.

Jenna took a moment to respond. "I guess I feel bad that you guys might have gone through this in secret. Alone."

Adam clinked his friend's wine glass filled with mineral water. "You're focusing too much on the past, Jay." He blew a kiss to a toilet-bound Maddy on the other side of the room. "The future's where it's at."

"Well at least we can be sure you made up the e-mails with the baby, ay?" declared Boyd. "How the hell do you come up with stuff like that, O'Doherty?"

Adam shrugged. "It wasn't that difficult."

*

From: "Adam O'Doherty" <edam_odoh@fathertobe.com>
To: "Tin Lid" <womb@almighty.com>
Subject: Par-tay

...My speech at the end of the night gave out a lot of thank-you's, but there was one that couldn't be done then and there.

Thank you, B.

It is the understatement of the ages, but I could not have achieved this without you. The miracle of our connection has not only permitted me to sample the divine on a daily basis, it has become the vehicle that saw my dream transformed into a miracle of its own. I look forward to repaying you the best that I can in the many years that lay ahead of us.

Thank you again.

Dad

p.s. Did you receive my last two messages? I ask because I still have received no reply. I know you're quite busy in there (I read you can get hiccups for up to twenty minutes at this stage of the pregnancy), but if there is a problem with our 'system', I'm sure it's best dealt with at your end. I doubt any technician in the Yellow Pages would be qualified to deal with a glitch in the Almighty's domain!

Let me know that you are receiving my mail.

*

From: "Adam O'Doherty" <edam_odoh@fathertobe.com>
To: "Tin Lid" <womb@almighty.com>
Subject: Hello?

Well, *The Umbilical Word* is already guaranteed to sell a dozen copies...

*

All eyes in the room fell upon him. He coughed. In these post-Immaculate Misconception days, Adam's Thursday night job description was clear—Designated Provider of Ante-Natal Class Entertainment and Diversion. The latter provision was the requirement right now. But what could he do? The just concluded viewing of Dawn Marks' personal birth video had, he feared, robbed him of speech for life. Maddy patted her husband's shoulder and winched herself up into standing.

"Everybody, before moving off for a supper I know we're all very much looking forward to now, I just wanted to let you know of the wonderful news that has come by us of late."

There was an audible exhalation from the gallery. In their moment of desperate need, and with Old Faithful Adam looking more geezer than geyser, Maddy had stepped in and rescued the moment. They were quite a team, the O'Doherty pair.

"My gorgeous handsome man here has recently discovered the way to make your dreams come true."

"Write a book about it!" shouted Brendan Carter. He and wife Barbara were having twins. This was his longest spoken sentence in three weeks of classes.

Maddy clicked her fingers.

"There might be something in that!"

*

From: "Adam O'Doherty" <edam_odoh@fathertobe.com>
To: "Tin Lid" <womb@almighty.com>
Subject: Hello?

...A number of the group wanted to give me money for the novel right then and there. I told them it might be wise to wait until the story is actually completed.

Which hopefully could be soon. Work has now officially begun on the edited draft of *The Umbilical Word*. Jim Fox has taken the job on himself. He says as a reader he's really enjoying it because he can relate to it...

*

"My two boys came after years of tests, cycles, drugs, herbs, lotions, acupuncture and fortune tellers, all of it trying to solve the sad riddle of 'Non-Specific Infertility'. In the end, the lads were the result of IVF."

The chief editor of Hutton House tucked the wrinkled, faded baby photo back into his wallet. Across from Café AIX, on the city-side footpath of Merthyr Road, a woman wearing a baby sling turned her back to the westerlies whipping through the bus stop.

"Christ, we were lucky. Quite a few people we knew ended up with nothing to show for all their effort." Jim Fox tipped his chinotto bottle toward Adam. "Have you figured out what your couple will end up with?"

Adam flicked through the manuscript—stamped with post-it notes, thinner than it ought to be—sitting between their half-finished lunches.

"Happily ever after," he said.

*

From: "Adam O'Doherty" <edam_odoh@fathertobe.com>
To: "Tin Lid" <womb@almighty.com>
Subject: Hello?

...I got a technician in yesterday to look at this computer, just for the hell of it. The verdict was that it's 'running so good you can keep it for your kid to use in the future'. I promised I'd ask you.

Would you like us to keep it, B?

Please let me know that my messages are getting through to you. It's now going on two weeks since your last contact. You don't have to write a long reply; a short note would be fine. Just so that that your overly-paranoid father can sleep a bit easier!

Love

Dad

20

From: "Adam O'Doherty" <edam_odoh@fathertobe.com>
To: "Tin Lid" <womb@almighty.com>
Subject:

Still no reply.

In the aftermath of my lapse at the hospital, you said you trusted me. Has that situation changed? Has fear overridden your trust? Do you feel like your words count for nothing now that I have my own words to contend with? If this is the barrier to our continued communication then let me remove it.

You are not in competition with this new life. You should not see writing as the enemy. Its purpose isn't to deny you of your father's time and attention.

The truth of the matter is this: it is not meant to deny you *anything*.

I believe to be a good parent, one must have a good sense of self. The TV talk shows are spilling over with marriages harbouring hollow lives and unrequited dreams. Invariably, the children become the source of redemption. Hardly fair, is it? Already faced with the challenge of finding meaning and value in their own existence, the kids are lumped with the impossible task of doing the same for their creators.

One month ago, I was sentencing you to such a fate. Today you are free.

Understand that I am writing *The Umbilical Word* not just for me, but for *you*.

*

From: "Adam O'Doherty" <edam_odoh@fathertobe.com>
To: "Tin Lid" <womb@almighty.com>
Subject:

Is it my fault?

Have I done something to upset you? Perhaps you feel I betrayed your confidence by taking our words to the world?

I realised only yesterday, when re-reading the last few e-mails, the full potential for you to feel this way. When the book breakthrough occurred, I was cognizant of the way Maddy might react having private fare dished up for public consumption. But I totally forgot about your stake in all of this. I did thank you earlier, and I truly meant what I said about paying you back in the years to come. But I now understand this may not be enough—there may be a need for immediate restitution.

This is *your* story, as much as it is mine and Maddy's. And you have every right to feel aggrieved if things are being shared that you feel ought to be kept between us. If this is the cause of our lapse in contact, then I'm sorry. I will do everything I can to make sure you feel comfortable with the public persona of *The Umbilical Word*.

I'm doing my best to mask my misgivings around Maddy, but it's difficult. I don't think she senses any concerns in me, and if she does she probably thinks it's to do with how the story is coming along.

Please send some word through, B.

For your mother's sake as well as mine.

*

Adam stared at the three marketing women seated opposite. They had fallen silent. Their wet-lipped, fake-tanned faces held expectation and enquiry. Adam rubbed his eyes and pushed to arm's length the pulsating urge to sprint for the spare room.

"I'm sorry. What did you say?"

"I said 'It's not just about *The Umbilical Word*. You're very marketable, too'," replied Soserina, twirling an index finger through bobbed Sunsilk strands.

"The book obviously has plenty of scope," forwarded Sydney, "and naturally all strategies will be explored."

"National ads, national tour, flyers, posters, teasers, postcards," added Bailey, counting off her manicured talons. "Even an online chat room where you can 'talk' to B!"

"But you're very marketable, too," repeated Soserina.

"You won't be forgotten," assured Sydney.

"How could we forget you?" chirped Bailey.

"Passionate but sensitive."

"Ambitious but friendly."

"Focused but balanced."

"Loves his wife."

"Loves his life."

"Loves the child he is yet to see."

The marketing trio exchanged glances and smiled. "The man every woman wants!" they cried.

Adam blinked once, twice, then looked up at the ceiling.

He was in deep shit.

*

From: "Adam O'Doherty" <edam_odoh@fathertobe.com>
To: "Tin Lid" <womb@almighty.com>
Subject:

What can I do to make you connect with me again, B?

Maybe nothing. Maybe my promises to make good can't make up for past sins. Maybe I am no longer worthy of the miracle. If that's the situation, then so be it. I have made my bed, I must lie in it.

But don't force your mother to lay beside me.

She should not have to suffer as I am suffering now. She should not have to contend that my gloom is the result of something other than my story. She should not be subjected to needless worry because my lack of respect compelled you to withdraw.

Send *her* a message. Honour *her* with the miracle. Spare *her* the awful suggestion that your silence with me is the result of something beyond my unworthiness.

Please, B—send Maddy a message.

Please.

21

Dawn Marks assisted Maddy into a sitting position on the bench. She then performed a small round of applause.

"No irregularities in shape or size, heart rate or position. You're all set for the home stretch."

Maddy smiled and hugged the midwife.

"So there's nothing going on that might be…a concern?"

The women broke from their embrace. They observed Adam replace *What to Expect When You're Expecting* back on the wall shelf.

"There's nothing to overtly suggest a threat to healthy delivery in approximately eight weeks time," comforted Dawn.

Adam turned his attention to his wife. "Has there been any change in the kicking, any lessening of movement?"

Maddy narrowed her gaze then spoke to her belly. "Kiddo, your Dada has been hanging around your Mama for too long. Now *he's* got the worry-warts!"

"Maddy, please let-"

"Relax Adam! We've come too far for anything to go wrong now, gorgeous handsome man. Way too far."

*

From: "Adam O'Doherty" <edam_odoh@fathertobe.com>
To: "Tin Lid" <womb@almighty.com>
Subject:

...Without any relieving message, to your mother or myself, how can I truly believe that you are beyond danger?

How can I have faith in unexplained loss?

*

"What's up with you, fella?"

Adam swung the Toyota onto bustling Brunswick Street. To the right, the Empire Hotel shimmied and shook under the heavy hand of an Acid House sampler. To the left, the footpath fronting The Zoo wore the screams of a council jackhammer. The combined caterwaul allowed Adam to wait two city blocks and one full minute before responding. He was grateful.

"I'm having a few hassles with the 'child' parts of the story."

Maddy watched the graffiti and the commercial real estate 'For Sale' signs slide by.

"Well snap out of it."

Red lights at the Village Twin intersection brought the four wheel drive to idle. Adam turned on the radio. Maddy turned it off.

"You've waited a long time for days like these, Adam O'Doherty," she said, twisting her expanse and wrestling with the seatbelt. "Don't spend them dwelling on stuff that will inevitably sort itself out."

They rode the dip down to Merthyr Road in silence.

At some point before reaching home, Adam opened the driver-side window and leaned toward the gusts of passing air, hoping they might take the moisture from his eyes and the golf ball lump from his throat.

*

From: "Adam O'Doherty" <edam_odoh@fathertobe.com>
To: "Tin Lid" <womb@almighty.com>
Subject:

...Could your mother survive the worst this time around? I honestly don't know.

Could *we* survive?

I don't know that either.

Tomorrow is my final day at school, probably my final day as a teacher. There are all sorts of tributes and salutes being organised, from a student concert in the morning to a staff roast in the afternoon.

I think I'm going to be sick.

22

From: "Adam O'Doherty" <edam_odoh@fathertobe.com>
To: "Tin Lid" <womb@almighty.com>
Subject:

Jim Fox informed me that everything is set for *The Umbilical Word's* first tentative steps into the world of literary expectation. Hutton House's publishing schedule has been shuffled around. The 'Coming Soon!' ads are ready for release. A profile of 'Adam O'Doherty—The Next Big Thing' is about to be set loose amongst the national media. Draft covers are being drawn up as I write. There's only one thing holding the process up.

The Umbilical Word needs an ending.

How is it to end, B?

23

Maddy entered the spare room and switched the meandering ceiling fan off. She was attired in the clothes that had become synonymous with this space—navy pedal pushers with ultra-expandable waist, Mambo Goddess tee stained by the sap of the backyard banana tree, stretched Roots quarter socks and squeaky Masseur sandals. She wore nothing else during the four and a half week transformation of the room. The nursery was the result of this uniform's small but honest toil. Love's labour had been absorbed into the fabrics, never to be excised.

She approached the ergonomic chair and, after several stress tests, lowered her full weight onto the velour seat. The computer desk had been Adam's exclusive preserve of late, despite her co-habitation of the room. Maddy had hardly given the station a second look during her days of daubing and dolling, pasting and pottering. Today she consumed its detail. The empty beer bottle standing by the mouse pad. The web-cam pointing toward the wall. The clumps of paperclips nestled in amongst the microphone wires. And the manuscript. Stacked and adjusted. Dead centre of the desk. Laying before the monitor like a holy offering. Giving every impression of a finished article.

Maddy cradled the mouse and clicked the net icon. As 'Logging On' scarpered down to the taskbar, she typed in her author husband's brand new username and password.

*

From: "Jenna Grimson" <grimsontide@hotmail.com>
To: "Adam O'Doherty" <adam@theumbilicalword.com>
Subject: Howdy!

Hey Boy

Wow! Love the webpage! Do you know how I found out about it? It was being advertised on the 'Pregnancy, Birth and Baby Expo' site! This book's really going to be something else when it hits the shelves. Can't wait to go up to a complete stranger thumbing through it in a store and tell them 'I'm the faker in that!'.

So, how is this perfect life treating you? Perfectly, no doubt (how ironic). I gather you're not getting out much at the moment, trying to finish off the story. I 'm sure it will work out brilliantly.

You're missed at school. You're still the hot topic of the lunch table (my pregnancy can't compete). Even The Sarge mentioned you the other day. Apparently he's been writing a thriller loosely based on his tours of duty in Vietnam for some years now. He said when it hits two hundred thousand words, he might get your opinion on it.

The kids miss you, too. Your friend Dregs is having a hard time coming to terms with your career change. He must think you were a pretty good teacher because he is adamant you're letting your child down by becoming a famous writer. I assured him that your child is fully supportive of your move, but he wasn't convinced. Maybe it has something to do with the fact that your replacement does a pretty good impression of one Callum Cuthbert Morecroft, pre-Strictly Ballroom.

Well, I should probably go for now. Boyd is hassling me to get ready. He found some cheap second-hand baby baths in the Trading Post and we're going to road test them.

These lives we're living, Adam...are you positive they really belong to us?

Of course yours does—YOU NAILED IT!

BOLA

Jay

p.s. See you at the last ante-natal class on Friday!

*

From: "Kelly Clark" <Wimble-Bum@hotmail.com>
To: "Adam O'Doherty" <adam@theumbilicalword.com>
Subject: Percentage of royalties, please...

Recluse Ed

Heard you were having some dramas coming up with an ending to your story, so I took the liberty of doing the job for you.

Father-to-be and his devilishly handsome friend are having a game of tennis. Friend is, as per usual, kicking Dad's arse when the pregnant wife rolls up and says she's going into labour. They jump into Dad's car only to find a stray ball (no doubt one of Dad's backhands...but, hey it's your story, you can choose any stroke you like) has pierced the bonnet and completely destroyed the engine. With no other transport, it's obvious Mum is going to have to give birth right here and right now. But where? Where can such a momentous event be conducted with dignity and decorum?

Friend spies the umpire's chair and...

I think you could fill in the blanks from here. Just make sure the devilishly handsome joker goes on to win the Australian Open with a bag of flour as his doubles partner.

Fear not, Ed—it'll all come together the way it should.

Don't be a stranger.

Love and fondles

Kel

*

From: "Tammy Turner" <witchway@hotmail.com>
To: "Adam O'Doherty" <adam@theumbilicalword.com>
Subject: Easy Ride From Here On In

Dear Adam

Just a short note to say I'm glad my interpretation of your cards was wrong. From what's happened in the last couple of months, it seems you were destined to be on the roller-coaster for a little while, but not all the way. No more loop-de-loops now, eh?

Keep smiling and keep taking care of your little family.

*

From: "Eileen and Reg O'Doherty" <eileenandreg@hotmail.com>
To: "Adam O'Doherty" <adam@theumbilicalword.com>
Subject: Hi from Mum and Dad

Adam

Hi. How are you? We haven't seen you for a while. We know you are very busy at the moment (not half as busy as you will be soon though!), but hopefully you can have a night off soon to come and visit us.

Do you know Madeline's been talking a bit with your father about the nursery? Before you get all worried thinking the little one will be surrounded by State of Origin memorabilia, they're not discussing decorating! It's been more the practical stuff, which drill bit for this and what screw for that. Reg was worried she was doing too much, but she said she knows her limits only too well these days. And any of that tough stuff, well that's what Grandpas are for!

I've never seen that girl of yours looking more at peace with the world, Adam. I couldn't have imagined it when she was in the hospital. She's going to make a wonderful mother. You really are a lucky boy to have her.

And we are very lucky to have you, Mr Writer! Michelle and Christopher, too. The Almighty has been very good to us, especially of late. Those extra prayers must have done the trick.

And, of course, we won't stop until the best little blessing of all has arrived!

Hope to see you soon.

Love

Mum

*

From: "Jenna Grimson" <grimsontide@hotmail.com>
To: "Adam O'Doherty" <adam@theumbilicalword.com>
Subject: Okay?

Ad

How's it going, bud? Is everything alright? You were awfully quiet at the last ante-natal class (certainly a lot more quiet then you were at the first one!). You seemed very distracted, like a hitman was after you or something. Is the story still giving you gyp? I hope it's that and not something else.

It's not something else is it?

Don't listen to Boyd if he tells you you've seen Woody Allen's *Love and Death,* too many times. Just because everything's going great in your life, that *doesn't* mean you then get an overwhelming urge to commit suicide.

Talk to me, Ad.

Jay

*

From: "Michelle O'Doherty" <docinwaiting@hotmail.com>
To: "Adam O'Doherty" <adam@theumbilicalword.com>
Subject: The Decider

Brud

Having a wee break from the books and thought I'd drop you a line to make sure you're still alive.

How are things travelling with the story? Almost finished? I guess the delays you're experiencing couldn't possibly be long enough to give me a chance at that episiotomy. So, with my concession that the score is now 1-1, I think it's time we settled on a decider.

How about 'First one to have a complete breakdown and lose it all'?

Take care

Shell

*

From: "Dilip Shastrani" <dilshas@hotmail.com>
To: "Adam O'Doherty" <adam@theumbilicalword.com>
Subject: Karma

Adam

I saw the sequel to *Karan Arjun* last night—Nasty Uncle's *karma* is to return as a rainstorm that saves Karan Arjun's town from a terrible fire—and I couldn't help thinking of you.

How are you enjoying *your* karma, my friend? Many people think 'karma' means payback or poetic justice. You do something bad and that bad returns to you. But karma actually means 'what is destined'.

I remember our chat some time ago when you spoke of miracles. Am I correct in thinking you foresaw the events that have since occurred? Indian legend contains stories of men who glimpsed their future, their *karma*, were willing to accept it and be grateful for it, and were looked upon favourably by the gods as a result. These men were very special and very rare. They are still regarded to this day as teachers for all the rest of us struggling with the outswingers life throws our way.

I have a question for you: Are you sure you're not Indian?

I apologise for not writing more, but it is my karma to pick up the pizzas we have ordered for dinner.

Stay happy my friend. You deserve all you receive.

Dilip

*

From: "Samantha Pole" <sampole@hotmail.com>
To: "Adam O'Doherty" <adam@theumbilicalword.com>
Subject: Thank You

Hi Adam

I just wanted to e-mail and say thank you.

I never made physical contact with Maddy and I've never read your book, but the strength and courage of both of you still must have rubbed off on me somehow.

I'm pregnant.

Thank you for being living proof that two miracles were indeed possible.

*

From: "Jenna Grimson" <grimsontide@hotmail.com>
To: "Adam O'Doherty" <adam@theumbilicalword.com>
Subject:

Adam

I had a chat to Maddy this morning and I found out things with you are a whole lot worse than a few unreturned e-mails and phone messages. She said you're like a ghost at home. You hardly talk, you look down in the mouth all day. The only time you come away from the computer is for meals, when she's working on the nursery, and to go to the loo.

That isn't the way I envisaged your dream come true, Ad. I'm pretty sure it's not the way you envisaged it either.

It's not the story doing this. There is something else going on isn't there.

What the hell is it?

And for God's sake, let Maddy know.

*

The whiny grumble of the Rav 4 filtered through the closed window and the floorboards. Maddy sat upright on the chair, fingering the smooth hematite stone in her necklace. There was no urgency or concern, none of the staple, startle responses associated with the pre-sprung trespasser. She felt only opportunity. The slow footsteps on the stair—*Tub... Tub...Tub*—might've been listless or methodical. At the top, they went dead. Five minutes passed. Maddy closed her eyes.

"You went out to clear your head, fella," she whispered. "Come in and do the same."

Car horns tooted in the gridlock three blocks away. An earthmover beyond the back fence prepared the way for another once-in-a-lifetime sprawl of units. A stream of Italian monologue sailed out of the neighbour's bathroom window, its pitch instructive, weighty. It sounded like a voice of reason.

Noises on the front deck. A whump. A bump. The rattle of keys, but not with intent. The clackety-clack of blinds drawing. The drag of a cheap outdoor chair across cheap wooden decking. The creaks and sighs of hinges as the canvas seat bears the full load of a burdened man. Then silence once more.

Maddy folded her arms. She bade goodbye to Jenna Grimson's most recent unanswered mail and clicked 'Compose'.

"God's sake not enough either," she murmured.

24

From: "Madeline O'Doherty" <maddymummy@hotmail.com>
To: "Adam O'Doherty" <adam@theumbilicalword.com>
Subject: Us

My Husband

I am writing this e-mail because, right now, I feel it is my best chance of you understanding what must be said. But it is the only one I am going to write.

In a few short weeks, things will change forever. We will enter the most important time in our marriage, the most important time in our lives. We're not perfectly prepared for what's to come—no one ever is—but at least we're going in with some things that will serve us well throughout the journey: devotion and strength and compassion and resiliency.

And each other's love.

I have a story for you. I've included it below—'The Legend of Siwash Rock'. Do you remember Siwash Rock from when I took you to Vancouver? It's that big boulder sitting all by itself in the shallow water of the Narrows, on the edge of Stanley Park. My mother told me the tale when I was seven, but the words following are not hers, nor mine. They belong to a writer.

I believe this is something you must read, Adam.

Before it's too late.

The Legend of Siwash Rock

It was thousands of years ago that a handsome boy chief journeyed in his canoe to the upper coast for the shy little northern girl whom he brought home as his wife.

Boy though he was, the young chief had proved himself to be an excellent warrior, a fearless hunter, and an upright, courageous man among men. His tribe loved him, and his enemies respected him, and the base and mean and cowardly feared him.

The customs and traditions of his ancestors were a positive religion to him, the saying and the advices of the old people were his creed. He was conservative in every rite and ritual of his race. He fought his tribal enemies like the savage that he was. He sang his war songs, danced his war-dances, slew his foes, but the little girl-wife from the north he treated with the deference that he gave his own mother, for was she not to be the mother of his warrior child?

The year rolled round, weeks merged into months, winter into spring, and one glorious summer at daybreak he wakened to her voice calling him. She stood beside him, smiling.

"It will be today," she said proudly.

He sprang from his couch of wolf-skins and looked out upon the coming day: the promise of what it would bring him seemed breathing through all his forest world. He took her very gently by the hand and led her down to the water's edge.

"I must swim," he told her.

"I must swim, too," she smiled, with the perfect understanding of two beings who are mated. For, to them, the old custom was law – the custom that the parents of a coming child must swim until their flesh is so clear and clean that a wild animal cannot scent their proximity. If the wild creatures of the forests have no fear of them, then, and only then, are they fit to become parents.

So those two plunged into the waters of the Narrows as the grey dawn slipped up the eastern skies and all the forest awoke to the life of a new, glad day. Presently he took her ashore, and smilingly she crept away under the giant trees. "I must be alone," she said, "but come to me at sunrise: you will not find me alone then."

He smiled also, and plunged back into the sea. He must swim, swim, swim through this hour when his fatherhood was coming upon him. It was the law that he must be clean, spotlessly clean, so that when his child looked out upon the world it would have the chance to live its own life clean. If he did not swim hour upon hour his child would come to an unclean father. He must give his child a chance in life; he must not hamper it by his own uncleanliness at its birth. It was the tribal law – the law of vicarious purity.

As he swam joyously to and fro, a canoe bearing four men headed up the Narrows. These men were giants in stature, and the stroke of their paddles made huge eddies that boiled like the seething tides.

"Out from our course!" they cried as his lithe, copper-coloured body arose and fell with his splendid stroke. He laughed at them, giants though they were, and answered that he could not cease his swimming at their demand.

"But you shall cease!" they commanded. "We are the men of the Sagalie Tyee, and we command you ashore out of our way!"

He ceased swimming, and, lifting his head, defied them. "I shall not stop, nor yet go ashore," he declared, striking out once more to the middle of the channel.

"Do you dare disobey us," they cried, "we, the men of the Sagalie Tyee? We can turn you into a fish, or a tree, or a stone for this; do you dare disobey the Great Tyee?"

"I dare anything for the cleanliness and purity of my coming child. I dare even the Sagalie Tyee Himself, but my child must be born to a spotless life."

The four men were astounded. They consulted together, lighted their pipes, and sat in council. Never had they, the men of the Sagalie Tyee, been defied before. Now, for the sake of a little unborn child, they were ignored, disobeyed, almost despised. The lithe young copper-coloured body still disported itself in the cool waters; superstition held that should their canoe, or even their paddle-blades, touch a human being, their marvellous power would be lost. The handsome young chief swam directly in their course. They dared not run him down; if so, they would become as other men.

While they yet counselled what to do, there floated from out of the forest a faint, strange, compelling sound. They listened, and the young chief ceased his stroke as he listened also. The faint sound drifted out across the waters once more. It was the cry of a little, little child. Then one of the four men, he that steered the canoe, the strongest and tallest of them all, arose, and, standing erect, stretched out his arms towards the rising sun and chanted, not a curse on the young chief's disobedience, but a promise of everlasting days and freedom from death.

"Because you have defied all things that come in your path we promise this to you," he chanted. "You have defied what interferes with your child's chance for a clean life, you have defied us when we would have stopped your swimming and hampered your child's future. You have placed that child's future before all things, and for this the Sagalie Tyee commands us to make you for ever a pattern for your tribe. You shall never die, but you shall stand through all the thousands of years to come, where all eyes can see you. You shall live, live, live as an indestructible monument to Clean Fatherhood."

The four men lifted their paddles and the handsome young chief swam inshore; as his feet touched the line where sea and land met he was transformed into stone.

Then the four men said, "His wife and child must ever be near him; they shall not die, but live also."

They, too, were turned into stone.

And if you penetrate the hollows in the woods near

Siwash Rock you will find a large rock and a smaller one beside it. They are the shy little bride-wife from the north, with her hour-old baby beside her.

From the uttermost parts of the world vessels come daily throbbing and sailing up the Narrows. From far trans-Pacific ports, from the frozen North, from the lands of the Southern Gross, they pass and repass the living rock that was there before their hulls were shaped, that will be there when their very names are forgotten, when their crews and their captains have taken their long last voyage, when their merchandise has rotted, and their owners are known no more. But the tall, grey column of stone will still be there – a monument to one man's fidelity to a generation yet unborn – and will endure from everlasting to everlasting.

E Pauline Johnson-Tekahionwake

Whatever has confronted you of late, Adam—whether it's your writing or something else that is beyond my comprehension—don't let it deviate you from your path. Stay the course and keep swimming, so it can be washed away.

And we will be ever near.

Love. And Faith.

Your Wife

Any Last Requests?

25

Adam stood before the bathroom mirror. Despite the puffy bags under the eyes and the gaunt form of the cheeks, he was recognisable to himself again. The unkempt beard was gone. The hair, washed on consecutive days for the first time in two months, fell in its natural arc across his right eyebrow. His clothes were from the drawer rather than the floor.

He exited the bathroom, walked down the hallway and stopped at the threshold of the once-spare room. The transformation to a nursery-in-waiting was complete, save the computer and desk in the far right corner. They would be relocated this afternoon. It was his one allocated job.

He entered and moved toward the open window. With elbows resting on the ledge, he took a moment to observe the day of his reckoning. It was grey, cloudy. A brisk August westerly toyed with the antenna on the neighbour's roof. The roundabout that emptied into the final, flat sweep of James Street down toward Merthyr Road and the Powerhouse contained no traffic. The cacophony of New Farm bustle, often a rasp in the throat of any sustained glimpse of outside, seemed distant, subdued. Adam closed the window and yanked the string of the drawn blind, sending the slats tumbling toward the ledge.

The unfinished manuscript lay on the left edge of the computer desk. Perched on top was the pewter lion-serpent. Adam twisted the souvenir until the creature's impassive gaze and gaping jaw faced the monitor. He looked around the room, pushed the ergonomic chair away from the desk, and clicked the mouse. 'The Umbilical Word' file came up on screen.

He placed a nearby cushion on the floor and knelt, both knees grounded, before the keyboard.

*

From: "Adam O'Doherty" <edam_odoh@fathertobe.com>
To: "The Almighty" <server@almighty.com>
Subject: We Need To Talk

Hello? Are you there?

I'm always here.

Can we talk like this?

It's not written in stone that you must kneel.

I thought it was. Regardless, I probably prefer it that way right now.

Then fire away.

I want to talk to you about...my future.

Always an important subject.

Is my future determined by you?

You choose the bus you ride. I provide the driver.

So this...bus I am on now, I have chosen it.

Absolutely. You hung your thumb out and everything.

Can I choose a different bus?

This one has your writing dream seated beside you. Why would you want to hop off?

Because perhaps others' journeys are more important than mine.

So it would not be your bus at all. It would belong to somebody else.

Can I choose it nevertheless?

Can you ring the bell? Of course! *But not until this current journey—your chosen journey—is complete*. It is complete when it pulls into station. At that time, the choice of a route is once again yours.

Do we have to keep using the 'bus' metaphor?

Writers like metaphor, don't they?

Not as much as their friends.

Would you prefer a train?

No, thank you.

As you wish.

Have I not already arrived at some point of change, of decision. Am I not standing at...okay, you win...a fork in the road?

No. You have presently encountered an opportunity to learn.

You mean a test.

I would've said a pothole...but if that's what you want to call it, go ahead.

Do I have to take it?

You sound like one of your former students, Adam! Put it this way—a note from 'Adam's Mum' won't help much.

You have created this test?

The opportunity to learn was always inherent in this journey.

So you *have* created this test.

Okay, okay, if it helps us move forward...then, yes, I came up with the questions, determined the marks, set the standard for a pass. I created this test.

*

Adam sat back on his heels. He chewed a thumbnail then inhaled through his nose. The air already carried the twin tinges of lanolin and talc. Like corner cobwebs, those smells could hang around in a room a long time. They could haunt a man's memory for longer still.

Adam lifted himself back onto his knees.

As he re-commenced typing, he failed to notice changes in the manuscript at his elbow. The lion-serpent now stood to the side of *The Umbilical Word,* facing the writer. Several of the manuscript's initial pages fell from the desk and settled in various locations on the nursery floor.

*

What if I refuse to take this test?

Ah, you want to be the defier, the stone warrior immortalised! The Siwash Rock legend is a wonderful story, isn't it? Sadly, though, it is not real life. The 'shy little bride-wife from the north, with her hour-old baby beside her', they were destroyed thirty years ago so that a concrete path could be laid down for tourists. The young husband and father now stands alone, his 'ever near' family sacrificed for the viewing pleasures of backpackers and grey nomads.

Are you saying I cannot refuse?

I am not the giants of the Sagalie Tyee. I will not become as other men if our courses collide.

Then I want to take a different test.

Do we have to keep using the 'exam' metaphor?

Can I take a different test?

I have already mentioned that what you are presently encountering is inherent in this pathway.

But as the creator of all pathways, could you not devise a new test? One that Maddy doesn't have to endure as well?

Maddy doesn't view this in the same way you do. She, like me, sees it as an opportunity to learn.

She hasn't experienced the miracle of our child's connection. And then had it taken away.

Hasn't she?

Not in the same way I have. She doesn't know what's coming.

And you do?

I think it has been made abundantly clear what lies ahead. And I am prepared to accept that it is my destiny. But why should innocents suffer?

History shows that it is inevitable.

Then create a new History! Start with Adam O'Doherty! Let him take a different test! One that doesn't affect others! One that can only affect *him*self and *his* dream!

You are thinking of *The Umbilical Word*.

Yes.

You would see it sacrificed?

I would.

For the sake of your child?

Yes.

'To be a good parent requires a good sense of self'—your words are they not?

I would re-define my sense of self.

What would you be?

A father.

So you wish to sentence your child to a lifetime of providing meaning and value for your existence as well as his or her own? You would let your child come to an unclean father?

Let me take a different test.

Adam---

Please.

It's not possible, Adam. I'm sorry.

*

Still kneeling, Adam laid his forehead on the desk. His right arm cradled his head. The left dangled and swung in front of his leaning torso, fingertips swiping the coarse calico of the cushion. The contact was like a serrated blade. After a dozen passes, the pendulum halted. He turned his hand palm-up, revealing the underside of the wedding band on his ring finger. Crafted into the gold surface was the tiny image of a wolf, symbolic of teaching, pathfinding and family.

Adam wedged the tip of his thumb under the ring and

levered. The loss of weight in the last two months now saw his fingers visibly thinner than in the days of a reliable miracle. The band slipped easily over the knuckle. It fell, bounced off the cushion and rolled under the cottage-style timber baby cot, positioned against the northern wall.

It came to rest on 'page 94' of *The Umbilical Word* manuscript. The previous ninety-three were distributed elsewhere across the nursery floor space.

*

Any last requests?

Watch over Maddy when this is done.

You wish that I should do your job?

I don't 'wish' for anything of the sort.

You don't trust her when she says she believes in you, and has faith in you, and that your love for each other will serve you well throughout this journey?

I feel this might be beyond the consolation of our love.

You have felt this way before, on three previous occasions. Your love stood firm.

We were blameless.

Maddy didn't think so. She blamed doctors, she blamed me and, ultimately, she blamed herself.

She was not responsible. Those tragedies were beyond anyone's control.

And you told her so.

Of course.

And you held her and comforted her and read to her, until she believed in the promise that things would be different next time around. You imagine such a treasured guardian of her dream would not be welcome in her future?

She deserves more than guardianship of her dream.

Any last requests for yourself?

End this quickly.

*

Adam stood and pivoted away from the computer. Sheets of printed A4 flew up from his feet. He checked where the manuscript had lain previously, on the left corner of the desk. Only blank pages remained. He scanned the room. The entire floor was concealed beneath *The Umbilical Word*.

"It will be today."

Adam looked up. Maddy stood at the entrance to the room.

She held an overnight bag in one hand and a bookmarked, purple paperback in the other. Her eyes glistened. The tears on her cheeks shone like diamonds from heaven.

Adam crossed the paper carpet between them and led his wife to the front door.

Hard Labour

26

From: "Adam O'Doherty" <adam@theumbilicalword.com>
To: "All Recipients"
Subject: Today

Dear All

I wanted to write a brief note to let you know where things stand.

The time is 9:52.

The day has passed.

Will there be another? In the wake of events that transpired during this sun-up, it's hard to imagine a new dawn. The night sky, visible from a window in Galbraith Private Hospital, Ward 4C, might have decided never to give way to morning light again. No more pain and tears and too much blood. Best to let people sleep eternal from now on, perchance to dream.

That won't happen. The sun will come up on a world beyond my comprehension. Maybe I'm just wishing for a return to the days before today.

I'm watching over her at this very moment, reading to her in my mind. She is pale and breathing quickly. The haemorrhage really knocked her around. They say she will need extra love tomorrow and that she won't be going home for a few days. I will be here the whole time, by her side, providing all the extra love she requires and more.

I'm not going anywhere.

Maybe she understands this, because she's smiling. Smiling like a pregnant teacher who no longer has to fake it, or a grandparent with puke on the clothes, or a Wimbledon champion making muffins out of his doubles partner, or a Med student on her first day, or a doctor worthy of a second miracle, or a writer afforded a happy ending to his story.

Dad reckons Mum's smiling because she's dreaming of the future.

He's okay, my Dad.

He calls me 'Miracle'.

Brendan Reginald O'Doherty

7lb, 3oz

Postscript

From: "Billy Lid" <womb@almighty.com>
To: "Adam O'Doherty" <edam_o'doh@fathertobe.com>
Subject: Um...Hello

Dear Dad

I'm not sure the way of the world ought to be questioned like this, but circumstances have persuaded me to put my hand up.

Hi. I'm your child.

You're probably surprised, maybe even shocked by my nosiness in contacting you at this early stage. You're probably thinking 'If this kid won't give me any peace eight weeks after conception, then we may as well have the feather-duster on hand in the delivery room'.

I'm sorry. It is not my intention to make you uncomfortable. That's the last thing I would want to do right now. I simply wanted to make sure there are no problems and, if we're in the clear, maybe you could give me a little preview of this merry-go-round called Life.

Are there any problems? Are you feeling good? Strong? Mum conceded yesterday that you were 'more stable' this time around. She's still nervous as all hell, but it warmed my heart to hear her say something positive. And Brendan, my brother, has had nothing but positives to say thus far. He reckons you were always 'too cool for school'.

Are you too cool for school?

Looking forward to your reply.

C

Other Fiction @ IP

As If!, *by Barry Levi*
ISBN 97818768194804, AU$30

Back Burning, *by Sylvia Petter*
ISBN 9781876819422, AU$28

The Buggerum Intrigue, *by Paul Sterling*
ISBN 9781876819682, AU$30

Easter at Tobruk, *by Michael O'Sullivan*
ISBN 9781876819405, AU$30

House of Given, *by Bill Collopy*
ISBN 9781876819378, AU$30

The Dispossessed, *by Andrew Lansdown*
ISBN 1876819308, AU$27

Secret Writing, *by Michael O'Sullivan*
ISBN 1876819294, AU$27

A Ticket for Perpetual Locomotion, *by Geoffrey Gates*
ISBN 1876819286, AU$27

The Diggings Are Silent, *by Wendy Evans*
ISBN 1876819243, AU$24

After Moonlight, *by Merle Thornton*
ISBN 1876819227, AU$25

Made in the USA